BOOK 6
in the
Second
Chances
SERIES

Falling Again

PEGGY BIRD

author of *Believing Again* and *Trusting Again*

CRIMSON
ROMANCE

F+W Media, Inc.

This edition published by
Crimson Romance
an imprint of F+W Media, Inc.
10151 Carver Road, Suite 200
Blue Ash, Ohio 45242
www.crimsonromance.com

ISBN 10: 1-4405-6976-2
ISBN 13: 978-1-4405-6976-0
eISBN 10: 1-4405-6977-0
eISBN 13: 978-1-4405-6977-7

With thanks to Jennifer Lawler, who took a chance on a new writer and brought the stories and characters of the "Second Chances" series to life. Or at least, to publication. You're the best.

Chapter 1

"He knows more than he told me. I can see it on his face. But how the hell can I get him to say it out loud?" Fiona McCarthy muttered to herself, frowning at the notes she'd hastily scribbled after her lunch with a just-departed Senate staffer. Her frustration at her inability to get more out of him was at stratospheric levels. If only she had the nerve to chase him across Capitol Hill and stick to him like a tick until he told her what she wanted to know.

She was enjoying the image of riding piggyback on the staffer, yelling her questions in his ear while he tried to go about his business, when a male voice interrupted.

"Fiona? I don't know if you remember me. We met about six months ago in Portland." The man belonging to the voice was standing beside her table, a leather jacket in one hand and a battered messenger bag slung over his other shoulder.

When she looked up she quickly shifted to what she hoped was a welcoming expression. "Of course I remember you, Nick. We met at your sister's house, Danny and Jake's engagement party."

She was not likely to forget him. Six-feet-something of broad-shouldered, slim-hipped male. Chestnut brown hair tamed with some sort of product to keep it tousled and in place at the same time. Carefully maintained fashionable stubble, which didn't manage to hide dimples when he smiled, as he was doing now. Sleepy, just-got-out-of-bed hazel eyes capable of melting the knees or any other part of a woman's anatomy.

Add a small gold hoop earring and a gold stud in his left ear, cargo pants he might have had tailor-made, a shirt setting off a better set of chest muscles than any she'd ever seen, (dressed or undressed) and if she hadn't known it before, she knew from seeing him she wasn't in Oregon any more. No one in Portland looked this good.

Ah, yes. Portland. Where her friend Amanda—his sister—lived. The sister who called him *baby* brother. The baby brother who was, from the way Amanda talked, barely out of his teens. Since Fiona didn't think she was old enough to qualify as a cougar, it meant her less than platonic thoughts about Nick made her a cradle robber. Not how she wanted to think of herself. Which was the important point to keep in mind; not how hot he looked.

It was also important to keep in mind how she'd met him. He'd blown into Oregon on an unannounced visit and proceeded to command—no, *demand*—the attention of everyone at a party he hadn't been invited to. Then, just before she left the party he'd done the "we should get together sometime" thing with her. Of course, he never asked how to get in touch with her. Not that she'd have given her number or address to him. Probably.

At the party he kept saying he didn't want to hog the spotlight, but he didn't do much to keep it from happening. Just like every other picture taker she knew, he thought his glamorous overseas assignments made him a star. Probably even a better reporter than the wordsmiths like her who pecked away at their computers all day in a nice safe office. The hell it did. Journalism wasn't about photographs; it was about words, stories that changed people's lives and opinions. If he wanted to move people with images, he should have majored in film studies.

Of course, if he had, his sexy good looks would have probably earned him an Oscar by now and she'd be even more annoyed with him.

Oops. He looked like he'd said something during her mental rant. "Sorry, it's noisy in here. I didn't quite hear you," she said trying to cover for her inattention.

"I said, I'm flattered you remember me," Nick said.

"Reporters never forget interesting people with fascinating jobs who might be a good source for a story someday," she said. *There. That should put him in his place.*

His smile turned into a semi-serious frown. "Ouch. I was hoping I was memorable for something more than my potential as an interview."

Was he really flirting? She couldn't believe it. "Doesn't 'interesting' and 'fascinating' count for something?" Waving at the empty chair across from her, she asked, "Have you had lunch? I'm finished, but if you'd like to join me…"

"I've eaten but I'll never turn down a cup of coffee with a beautiful woman." He draped his jacket on the back of the chair, sat and flagged down a server.

"How did you recognize me out of context?" Fiona asked. "I'm not always good at it." *Maybe if she led by example, he'd keep his ego at bay and his flirting on a low flame.*

After he ordered coffee, he answered her question. "It would be hard to forget you. The expression on your face when my niece asked during the toasts if Jake was going to plant a seed in Danny to make a baby is indelibly etched on my mind."

Something she, too, had to acknowledge wasn't easy to forget. "I thought you were the one who looked surprised."

With a sinfully sensuous smile he said, "No, I'd heard vague rumors about sex before then. Are you sure you weren't startled?"

"Not about sex—I've done a story or two about it in my career. Although I was surprised to find out how much four-year-olds know about the subject these days."

"I have a feeling my brother-in-law was not too happy with my sister for giving their daughter that little piece of information." The server interrupted, placing Nick's coffee in front of him with a flourish. "Are you in D.C. for business or pleasure?" he asked when the man was gone.

"A little of both. I was coming back east on vacation, for a wedding on the Eastern Shore of Maryland this weekend, in St. Michaels, and decided to make some appointments on Capitol Hill tracking down a couple stories. On my own dime, of course.

The paper barely pays for mileage to Salem to cover the legislature these days." *Unlike your foreign junkets, five star hotels, and fancy banquets with important people.*

"How long will you be here?"

"Not quite a week, broken up with the weekend in Maryland."

"I just got back in town from an assignment, but when I sort out my schedule maybe we could have dinner before you leave."

"You're sweet, but it's not necessary. You must have a ton of things to catch up on." *And none of them include amusing yourself with me.*

"It would be my pleasure. Not only do I eat dinner on a regular basis, but I prefer good company while I do. Do you have a favorite restaurant in town?"

"Actually, I usually end up eating at my hotel or having room service."

"If you give me your cell phone number, I'll call and we can expand your horizons."

For a half hour, until he had to leave for a meeting, they drank coffee and talked about the people they knew in common and their jobs—his as a photojournalist, hers as an investigative reporter for *Willamette Week*, Portland's alternative newspaper.

It was a good thing they were covering familiar ground because in spite of the fact he irritated her with his extra helping of self-assurance, Fiona couldn't deny how damn attractive he was, which made it hard to concentrate on what he was saying. He was a smart and entertaining conversationalist, all right. But she was more interested at *looking* at his mouth than in listening to what was coming out of it. With a voluptuous lower lip and a perfect Cupid's bow upper lip, it was a mouth she wouldn't mind having kiss her at the spot right behind her ear or the one at the base of her throat. She stifled a moan at the thought.

Oh, God. He licked a drop of coffee off his lower lip with the tip of his tongue. How could something so simple be so sexy?

Before she could rid herself of images of him tasting the inside of her mouth, his eyes caught hers with a look she could swear said he knew exactly what she'd been thinking. Which was not good.

And which switched her attention from his mouth to his eyes. With the longest eyelashes she'd ever seen on anyone—male or female—and the gold flecks flashing in the hazel, she could get lost there, too.

Dear God, there better not be a quiz on this conversation. I'll flunk for sure.

Even repeated silent reminders that he was Amanda's much younger brother couldn't whip her errant thoughts into some semblance of adult behavior. Well, the kind of adult behavior two grown-ups demonstrated in public. The other kind, the private kind, was what she wanted to suppress.

She tried mental math. She was thirty-two. He looked like he was in his twenties, which, from Amanda's comments about when he graduated from college, would make him maybe twenty-two or twenty-three. Being this attracted to someone who was practically a teenager felt…well, it felt naughty.

Or exciting.

Whoa, reining in imagination here.

Even if he had spent most of the party at Amanda's home chatting her up, she didn't think the reason was any more complicated than they'd been the only single people there and had related jobs. Even without the age thing, she was sure someone who traveled the world for his job would find a girl from Tacoma, Washington, who'd never been out of the country, fairly uninteresting. And then there was the "I'll call you" thing, which hadn't happened. Was it any more likely to occur this time?

She tuned back into the conversation in time for him to ask for her cell number, again, and to promise to call as soon as he got a couple things on his schedule straightened out.

As she watched him walk toward the door, Fiona reminded herself not to hold her breath waiting for the phone to ring. What was more important was digging the information she was after out of the staffers she would be talking to on the Hill. She went back to reviewing her notes, the sexy, young photographer relegated to the same place she'd put him after the party in Portland—to the back of beyond.

• • •

Nick St. Claire left the restaurant near Capitol Hill where he'd been listening to a pitch about a possible piece of work very, very pleased with himself. He'd arrived back in town two days earlier after covering another tribal clash in Indonesia. There wasn't much on his plate until his next assignment in a couple weeks other than the opening of a show of his work at a gallery in Alexandria. Then he got his usual "let's-check-on-baby-brother-Nicky" phone call from Amanda, and she casually mentioned Fiona's presence in D.C.

Amanda couldn't have known—at least he didn't think she knew—how her friend, the beautiful redhead with creamy skin and blue-gray eyes, had been his mental companion off and on during several recent photo shoots. Had he met Fiona any other way than through his sister, he'd have already followed up after the party last fall to scout out the territory. But he'd been reluctant. Getting involved with someone who was friends with his sister might not be such a good idea. Much to his dismay, Amanda still babied him, felt it her duty to comment on his life, and picked apart any of the women he dated who she met or heard about through the family grapevine. In short, she interfered to such an extent, he wasn't interested in having her know he found her friend attractive; wasn't sure how he could ever find a way to test the waters with Fiona to see how warm they were as long as she was in Portland where his sister was.

But Fiona was hard to forget. She was smart, she was funny, and she was great to talk to. Although he had to confess he wasn't exactly looking for interesting conversation at the moment. After a month of living in mud, eating bad food, and avoiding Toyota pickups full of roaming groups of armed rebels, he wanted something more basic: dinner at a nice restaurant with a beautiful woman followed by dessert in his bed. And Fiona might just fill the bill. Today, even in the Ms. Business Professional black suit with the lacy bit under her jacket modestly covering up her cleavage, he could see curves he wouldn't mind exploring further.

When Amanda said Fiona was on his turf, he decided he'd track her down if he had to call every hotel near Capitol Hill and stalk every restaurant hangout for legislative staffers. It turned out he didn't have to search anyplace. He ran into her as if it were meant to be.

He had her phone number. His sister was nowhere in sight. He'd have Fiona all to himself for a week. A week to play around with someone hot and sexy until he got back to his real life—the one occasionally featuring mud and armed rebels. Sometimes the planets aligned just right.

• • •

On her way out the door of the Hyatt on Capitol Hill next morning, Fiona's phone rang. Sure it was either a confirmation of an appointment or a cancellation; she hurriedly dug through her purse and pulled it out. The voice at the other end of the call was a surprise.

"Morning, Fee. It's Nick. It's not too early to call, is it?"

"No, your timing's good. I'm just on my way to the Hill."

"Are you free for dinner tonight?"

"Tonight? Oh, I'm sorry, I can't. I've got a reception to attend."

"Those things never have enough food to qualify as dinner. How about meeting after the reception?"

What the hell was going on? Why was he suddenly so anxious to see her? He hadn't bothered to contact her after they met in Portland. Why was he pushing to spend the evening with her in D.C.? There had to be some reason other than the need to eat dinner.

"This one always does. And you don't have to…"

"I told you—I want to. Please?"

As much as she hated to admit it, even through the phone the husky timbre of his voice sent shivers up her spine. "How about you join me at the reception? It's open to guests. Put on by a group from the Northwest. They invite press people from all over the Northwest every year along with the entire delegation. They put on a good show I hear; lots of regional wine and smoked salmon, among other things. I've always wanted to attend and this year not only am I in town but I have an excuse. Some of my contacts will be there."

"Good smoked salmon? I'm there. Where and what time?"

"It's in 902 in the Hart building. I'll be there about six-thirty."

"Hart building—on the Senate side?"

"Yeah, the ever popular Hart SOB—Senate Office Building."

"Meet you there and then we can have dinner after."

"It might be late getting out."

"It's okay. I've been allowed to stay up past nine for the past year or so. See you tonight."

She closed her phone, threw it in her purse, and walked toward the Hill, her step as snappy as the sound the flags on the Capitol made as they rippled in the spring breeze. It had taken way too long to get past the debacle of her last relationship. Maybe the attention of a sweet young thing might be exactly what she needed for a warm-up before she threw herself into the dating game again. Even if said sweet young thing was a bit arrogant and way too sure of himself.

Now, if only her appointments worked out as well.

Chapter 2

Thank God for the dinner invitation from Nick, Fiona thought as she schlepped back to her hotel. It was the only thing saving the day from being a complete waste of time. She'd talked to at least a half dozen staffers in the offices of Oregon's delegation on Capitol Hill, but her failure to get something useful on the stories she was chasing continued unabated.

Everyone gave her the press release version of the first story she was researching, a piece about a bill Congressman Dick Anderbock, the most conservative member of the delegation, had recently introduced. The legislation would encourage coal and natural gas development by loosening environmental regulations as long as the coal was mined with equipment manufactured in the United States, used domestically or, if exported, shipped out of U.S. ports using ships registered in the United States. The last requirement was currently hanging up a committee vote on the bill while staffers scrambled to find out if there were any bulk carriers flying the U.S. flag to carry the coal.

Supported by some loud voices in the Portland business community and several members of the City Council, it was—not surprisingly—opposed by most of Oregon's environmental organizations. Fiona had talked to their lobbyists before she got to Washington. What she was trying to ferret out was an intelligent opinion—okay, *anyone's* opinion—on the bill's chances in the Senate, as passage in the House was a given.

Fiona had pushed and prodded at her contacts on the Hill, bringing up the governor's recent initiative on green businesses, his move to reduce the carbon footprint of businesses in the state, trying to get them to comment on how his goals fit with the Anderbock bill. Either because they didn't want to get their bosses caught crosswise with another politician or because they didn't know the answer, the staffers she talked to fudged.

The passage of the Anderbock bill was the straightforward story she was following. The other one, about a white supremacist organization with the bizarre name of White Power Knights of the West, was murkier. Rumors were flying all over Portland about a group with a racist agenda about to go public and back candidates for local and state office. The rumor brought up uncomfortable reminders of Oregon's history in the early twentieth century when the state elected an active member of the Ku Klux Klan as governor and passed both sundown laws barring African-Americans from being in public after dark and laws banning religious dress for teachers in an attempt to close Catholic schools.

At the intersection of the two stories was a list of three businessmen who supported the Anderbock bill and who some in Portland believed might be the money behind the organization about to open offices in town. Their businesses explained their interest in the Anderbock bill. What she wanted was more information on the three men to uncover which, if any of them, was behind the mysterious organization. All she got was what she already knew.

J. Henson "Hen" Ondsdorph was the head of New Power, Inc., a company with controlling interest in one of the region's investor-owned utilities with extensive coal holdings. For years he'd worked on a variety of ways to exploit the resource, including plans to develop an Oregon port so he could ship coal to China.

Wallace Wellington, known as "Duke," made his fortune buying up farmland and having it rezoned for development just before Oregon's land use laws went into effect in the early seventies. Since then he had enjoyed using the profits to, as he liked to describe it, "steer the course of Oregon" in directions he favored. The local enterprises he backed included several manufacturers of power plant components.

The third man, Sherman Bischler, was from an Idaho family whose wealth went back to the silver mining days. His parents had moved to Oregon where his father started a company that manufactured mining equipment, which was exported all over the world from the company's headquarters in a suburb of Portland.

All three men had bankrolled the campaign of both Anderbock and the recently defeated incumbent mayor of Portland. And all three were known as conservative in their politics. However, "conservative" in Oregon didn't usually mean the holder of the opinions was rabid on race issues.

But something odd had happened today when she mentioned the rumors she'd heard about the white power organization to her contacts.

Silence. Nothing. No comments. No additional information. Not even acknowledgement they'd heard rumors, in some cases. Even dangling the names of the three business leaders who might be funding the group like treats in front of puppies didn't get her anything. Her instincts told her at least some of them knew more than they were willing to say about the three men. Were they hiding their employers' opinions? Were they protecting campaign contributors? Or were they up to their own skinny little necks in the new organization?

Not only had she gotten nothing, but she had run overtime not getting it. She only had enough time to dump her notebook, freshen her makeup, and decide whether to go strictly business in her choice of clothes or more social. She opted for the latter, replacing her jacket with a poet blouse, which had a portrait collar to frame her face and long, full sleeves with ruffles at the wrists to look flirty and feminine. She already had on silver hoop earrings and bangle bracelets. Wrapping it all up in a soft, woven stole in shades of blue-gray, black and white, she was headed back to the Hill in less than half an hour turnaround.

The reception was an annual event hosted by the Pacific Northwest Waterways Association, a regional group of ports, utilities, agricultural interests, and shippers. The food and wine served was from the region and the entire delegation from the Northwest, as well as other senators, representatives, and staff members showed up to eat, drink, socialize—and lobby. Fiona had been invited to the event before but had never been in D.C. to attend. Tonight she hoped to have better luck at getting some of the answers she was seeking than she'd had in office visits because it was a social event with free wine involved.

So busy was she making the rounds of staffers from various offices, she didn't notice Nick arrive. But when she saw a dozen or more young women looking across the room at something, or someone, she turned and saw him, just inside the entrance, scanning the room. For her.

He was dressed in gray pants, a white, open-collared shirt that fit his body like a glove, and a black, Ralph Lauren-looking jacket. The just-out-of-bed hair and the sleepy eyes were as impressive from across a crowded room as they were up close.

When he spotted her, he smiled and made his way through the crowd to her. "You're not hard to find, are you?" He leaned in and kissed her cheek.

She certainly hadn't expected that gesture. It made her fumble for a response. What came out was, "It's the red hair. There aren't many of us around. You were pretty easy to pick out yourself. All I had to do was look in the direction all the other women in the room were looking."

"You mean, all the people saying 'who the hell is the stranger who doesn't belong here'?"

"Your modesty is admirable." *If unbelievable*, she almost added before gesturing to follow her. "Let's get you a glass of wine and I'll introduce you to a few people."

An hour later, after sampling all the goodies and chatting with a few staffers and another reporter, Fiona noticed signs the reception was winding down. "Ready to leave?" she asked Nick.

"When you are. If you're still hungry, there's a little Mexican restaurant close by where we can have dinner. Or I know a great place where we can get dessert."

"I think dessert, and maybe an after dinner drink. I'm wound tight after a day of trying to pry information out of rocks."

"I noticed you weren't drinking wine on duty. The place I have in mind will be just right."

A short cab ride took them to the restaurant, where they ordered Irish coffees and desserts. After the server left, they sat in silence for several moments.

"Why is it," Fiona asked, "two people can have a great conversation when they just bump into each other, but they're silent when it's, you know, a date-like setting." She waved her hand and felt her face begin to flush. "I didn't mean to intimate this is a date but…" *Jesus, where was the filter on her tongue when she needed it? Two sips of Irish coffee shouldn't make her that stupid.*

"It's not? I thought it was. How'd I get it wrong?" He frowned, as if thinking hard. "Let me see—man asks woman out. Man shows up in his best blazer but no tie so he doesn't look like he is going to a funeral or a job interview. Woman has changed into non-business clothes and looks beautiful. Man has a selection of restaurants in mind to impress woman with his good taste and sophistication." He shook his head. "No, I got it right. This is a date."

She laughed. "I didn't want to seem presumptuous by assuming because you were nice enough to ask a friend of your sister's to have dinner that it's a date."

"I didn't ask you to dinner because you know Amanda. I asked because I wanted to see you again. And now having established we are, in fact, on a date, maybe we can move on. I'm curious about what you said about your day. Or is asking about your day either too date-like or not date-like enough? I don't want to make a mistake here."

"I think it's more like husband-and-wife-stuck-in-a-boring-rut."

"We blew right past date to husband and wife? God, woman, you move fast."

"Ignoring the insult…"

"I didn't mean it as an insult. I like fast women." He wiggled his eyebrows in a fake leer.

"Ignoring both insults and the eyebrow thing, my day was weird. Interesting, but weird. This story I'm trying to get a handle on keeps slipping through my fingers. It's all blue smoke and mirrors; nothing solid, nothing traceable. It's frustrating as hell."

"And your contacts on the Hill couldn't help?"

"Some swore they knew nothing. A few said they only heard rumors they weren't willing to repeat. But beyond that no one can—or is willing to—give me anything. They all clam up as soon as I push the subject. I have no hard facts, no source who'll go on record…"

"So, no story. You do have a problem."

The server returned with their drinks. Nick picked up his glass and touched it to hers. "To clearing away the smoke."

"I wish it was that easy. But then, I guess it would seem easy to someone who doesn't have to get people to open up to him to get their pictures taken."

"Interesting description of photojournalism. But you're right. I don't have to dig into their lives with my questions; I can get the images to tell the story. It's not always easy but…"

"But when you're as good at it as I hear you are I guess you don't have to worry."

The waiter arrived with their desserts. Nick looked across the table at hers. "I hear chocolate can be good for quelling the crazies caused by unresponsive sources. Let me know, will you?"

Fiona took a bite of her chocolate mousse cake and moaned. "This may be the answer to every problem I've ever had."

He grinned and offered her a bite of his bread pudding.

Dessert finished, Nick announced they should end their evening with a walk around his favorite place in the city. He flagged down a cab and asked the cabbie to take them to the Tidal Basin near the Jefferson Monument. It was one of her favorite places, too, which must be the reason she was letting this evening continue. She'd planned to thank him for the dessert and take a cab back to her hotel where her lovely—and empty—hotel room was waiting. Yet here she was, against her better judgment, hanging out with someone who might be spending the evening with her as a favor for his sister, was young enough to get her arrested for corrupting the morals of a minor, and who was hot as hell.

Unfortunately.

He took her hand as he helped her out of the cab and didn't let it go as they started walking. After a few minutes of sauntering through the unusually warm night in silence, he said, "You should know—I got credit yesterday I don't deserve."

"Oh, why?"

"I knew you were in town so you weren't exactly out of context when I saw you."

"How did you…?"

"Amanda. She calls me occasionally to meddle in my life. And always to make sure I get back safely from an overseas assignment. During the latest conversation she happened to mention you were here so I thought I'd use this chance to get to know you better without the interference of my loving but bothersome sister."

She stopped in the shadow of one of the cherry trees and looked up at him, her head slanted to one side. *He'd been looking for her? Why would he do that?* "Now I'm the one who's flattered. I'm not sure what to say."

"You don't have to say anything. Just let me do this…" He put his hand at the nape of her neck and drew her mouth toward his.

It was better than she'd imagined, having his mouth on hers. It was both sensuous and sweet, seducing her rather than demanding from her, making her want to give him what he was asking for even if she didn't understand why he was asking. He kissed her top lip, then her bottom lip, then coaxed them apart with his tongue. When he had adjusted his mouth on hers, finding the perfect fit between them, he used his tongue to taste the inside of her lips.

Her arms went to his shoulders and his arm circled her waist, pulling her close. She was on the verge of deciding she'd do just about anything to keep the kiss going when two teenaged boys on skateboards come whizzing past, cat-calling and making sucky-kissy noises. The mood was broken. They ended the kiss with laughter and continued their stroll in the moonlight.

At the hotel he asked if she would have dinner with him again the next night, since she'd be gone for the weekend and he couldn't see her. It must have been the moonlight or maybe the kiss. Probably both. Because she agreed to meet at seven the following night. He kissed her again, sealing the deal. As she went down the escalator into the lobby, she knew it wouldn't be too hard to get used to kissing Nick St. Claire. The question was, should she?

Chapter 3

The next day, Nick texted Fiona a couple times, asking about her day and whether she'd gotten one of her clams to open up, inquiring if there was any kind of food she hated and moving their meeting time to six-thirty. His messages were a pleasant change from what usually clogged her phone—breaking news alerts, which may or may not be news or alert-worthy, and boringly similar press releases boasting of some minor accomplishment someone wanted featured in the paper.

When she got back to the hotel at six she tried for the second time in a couple of hours to reach her boss but got voicemail again. Odd. Why wasn't he around? Maybe one of her colleagues would know. She started to make another call until she saw the time. She was running close to being late for meeting Nick, so she texted "where are you?" to her editor and moved to her next problem: what to wear.

Nick had said the night before was a date, but she was still unsure why, exactly, he was paying attention to her. To be honest, she was unsure why she was paying attention to him, other than the fact he was handsome, charming, and sexy. Which made him right for her attempt to get back on the horse, so to speak. Of course, that image only gave her impure thoughts about saving a horse and riding a cowboy. And that sure wasn't on the menu.

So she didn't want to come across as hot and ready for a tumble with a young stud. Given the clothes she had with her, the sexy look seemed out of her reach anyway. *Oh, hell, McCarthy, be honest. Even if you'd packed everything in your closet you couldn't pull off hot and sexy with someone so young.*

Finally she decided on the pale blue sleeveless silk dress and soft, unstructured jacket in a nubby fabric she'd planned to wear to the wedding. As she carefully reapplied makeup, she concluded she was making too much out of this. It was no big deal, at least not for him. It was merely dinner with a friend. Even though he said it was what he wanted to do, maybe Amanda asked him to be nice to her and he'd agreed because he'd enjoyed talking to her in Portland. Maybe. Although, come to think of it, maybe not. She doubted Amanda had asked him to kiss her. It was confusing.

After brushing her hair one more time, she took a last look in the mirror before heading for the elevator. She looked okay. If it was a favor for his sister, at least she wouldn't embarrass him. Riding down to the lobby she had to admit, regardless of his age or why he'd asked her out, she was looking forward to seeing him again.

He was waiting in the lobby. This time he wore the black leather jacket he'd been carrying the other day, gray pants, and a dark red T-shirt snug enough to show off his amazing pecs.

"You look nice," he said as he kissed her on the cheek.

"Thank you. You look quite nice yourself. Can I buy you a drink so we can class up the bar with our presence before we go to dinner?"

"I thought I'd give you a rare treat and take you to my place for a glass of wine before dinner, if it's okay with you. But I have to warn you, my place isn't much more than where I keep extra clothes between plane trips."

She laughed. "You make it sound like you live in a storage unit. Why are we going there if it's so inhospitable?"

"Self-protection. Once my sister knows—and she will find out—that we've had dinner a couple times she'll cross-examine you about my life. I want you to tell her you've been to my apartment and it's so well appointed I could be featured in some house and garden magazine. Or at least the style section of a small-town newspaper."

"She hasn't been here to see for herself?"

"Every time she tries, she gets diverted to Ohio by our mother who wants to see her only grandchild. It'll be up to you to satisfy her curiosity."

"And what makes you think I'll agree to take your side in a scheme to game my friend?"

"Because I can see in your eyes you're kind, and I can rely on you to feel sorry for me because I have such an intrusive sibling."

"Not exactly what I'd say I feel for you, but I guess I can at least reassure her it isn't rat and roach infested." She was sucked in again by the bedroom eyes and the sexy smile. "I…I mean, you are varmint-free?"

"I'm more interested in the first part of the sentence, the part about what you feel for me."

"I just meant I don't feel sorry for you, Nick."

"That's all?"

Damn. Would she ever figure out what this man was after? "Now I feel like I'm the one being played. Am I?"

He never answered the question with anything other than his smile, because the doorman opened the door to the cab he had hailed for them and helped her inside.

• • •

His apartment didn't live up to the bad press Nick had given it. On the second floor of a modest but newly renovated building near Dupont Circle, it consisted of a living area with a small kitchen, a bathroom, and one bedroom. The living room reminded Fiona a bit of the apartment she'd lived in right out of college—the couch was a futon, the extensive DIY bookcases overflowed with books. Only the two chairs grouped with the couch around a small table looked like they had come from a real furniture store.

But if the furniture wasn't outstanding, the accessories certainly were. The cloth on the small dining table as well as the rugs looked

Central American and the fabric covering the pillows on the futon was, she guessed, Thai silk. The walls were hung with beautifully framed photographs of colorful marketplaces, exotic landscapes, and people in ethnic dress—his work, she assumed. And he had electronic gear she would have killed for. On the dining table was the biggest MacBook she'd ever seen. On one bookcase shelf she saw a Bose dock with an iPod Touch, above the top shelf was a flat screen TV and there appeared to be an iPad and a Kindle on the table in front of the couch.

As she walked around the room, admiring each photograph, she said, "I think you were underplaying your apartment so I'd be wowed by it. Your photographs alone are amazing. I've always liked your landscapes in Amanda's dining room, but these are even more spectacular." She gestured toward the bookcase. "And your collection of electronic paraphernalia is truly impressive."

His grin acknowledged his pleasure. "Thanks. The art is from my first solo show at a local gallery a few years back. And the gear is an addiction. In addition to what you see, I have another TV in my bedroom and more camera equipment than any sane person should have, even one who makes his living with it. The guy who sold me renter's insurance couldn't believe I had so little furniture and so much other stuff, even when he saw it."

"So, great images on the wall, expensive—but insured— electronics, enough comfortable furniture to feel like home and not a rat or a roach in sight. Maybe not a candidate for a magazine spread but a nice place for a responsible grown-up to live. Sound like what Amanda needs to hear?"

"With an emphasis on the *responsible grown-up*, which she seems to forget I am."

"Are you serious? She'll ask?"

"She has fussed over me all my life. Part of it is, she loves playing big sister to her baby brother. Part of it is, she's a fusser. She'll ask."

Fiona started to ask how much of a baby brother he was but wasn't really sure she wanted to know so she kept quiet as she watched him pour two glasses of a very nice red wine. He handed one glass to her and motioned her to the futon.

During the course of drinking the wine the conversation turned to what Nick was working on. Fiona was unaccountably pleased when he told about an offer he'd had to shoot a story about recreation opportunities in the Cascade Mountains to begin after his next assignment in Canada. If he took the offer, he'd be in the Northwest for about two weeks, most likely based in Portland.

As they finished their wine, Fiona asked, "You said you'd made a list of places to eat to impress me with your good taste and sophistication. So where are we going tonight?"

"Should have known better than to try and slip a statement like that past a reporter. It's a Cuban place in Adams-Morgan. They have good food and good music. And we have a seven-thirty reservation."

The restaurant wasn't far and the evening pleasant so they walked. Nick took her hand as they started out, which she was surprised to find felt comfortable, as if they'd been a couple for a long time. Focused on his thumb caressing the back of her hand, she almost missed the greeting from a man who called her name as they crossed the street a block away from their destination.

"Oh, my gosh, Hank. How've you been?" She dropped Nick's hand and gave the man a hug.

The drivers trying to negotiate the intersection laid on their horns and made the three of them run for the sidewalk.

"I'm great," Hank said when they got to the sidewalk. "And you?"

"Same." She turned to her date. "Nick, this is Hank Lewis. He used to work for *Willamette Week,* and then moved up in the world to a gig with the AP here. Hank, Nick St. Claire."

"What are you doing just walking around town like you don't have a care in the world when there's a hot story back in Portland?" Hank asked.

"What hot story?"

"Haven't you had your phone on? What've you been doing for the last few hours?" He looked from Fiona to Nick with a knowing smirk.

"Come on, Hank, what's going on?"

"Guy fired two shots at the mayor during the City Council meeting today."

"You're kidding. Now I know why I couldn't find my editor this afternoon. Do they know who?"

"They got him. Some man named Preston Garland. The cops kept everyone in the building from leaving and the mayor and her chief of staff ID'd the guy. Cops arrested him on site."

"Not the smartest assassin in the world, apparently."

"No, but I heard he has interesting ties to some white power groups."

"Oh, shit. Come have a drink with us and tell me more."

"Love to," Hank said, "but I'm on my way to meet someone myself. We can talk in St. Michaels. I assume you'll be at the wedding tomorrow."

He said his goodbyes and Nick and Fiona continued down the block to their restaurant. They were immediately seated and Nick ordered glasses of wine for them.

Their server returned with their drinks and they ordered dinner—the arroz con pollo and ropa vieja Nick recommended. After the server left, she picked up her glass and took a sip.

"So," Nick said, "from what your friend says, things aren't the usual laid back and mellow in Portland."

When she returned the glass to the table, she held the stem in her hands and, staring into the bowl, twirled the glass between her fingers. "Awful, isn't it?" She moved restlessly in her chair. "I don't think anything like this has ever happened before."

He laughed. "You're dying to make a couple phone calls, aren't you?"

"I'd apologize for being so obvious, but I'm afraid terminal curiosity is an incorrigible part of my personality."

"And what makes you a good reporter. So make the phone calls. I'll have the waiter hold our meals for…what…ten minutes?"

"Make it fifteen, if you really don't mind." Although she tried to keep her expression under control, she was sure he could see excitement on her face about the hot story, mixed with relief she wouldn't have to wait to follow up on it.

"Believe me, I understand. Try being around me when the light is exactly at the right angle for the shot I've been stalking for a few days. I'd mow over my mother to get what I was after much less put off dinner with a date."

"You're terrific. Should I leave or…"

"No, no, no. Stay here, so I can eavesdrop."

He signaled to their waiter while she dug her cell phone out of her purse. She called around her office until someone answered the phone. When she found out Sam Richardson was one of the detectives in on the investigation she called him, too. Sam was the one cop who would always answer her calls—he was married to her friend Amanda and she'd done him a few favors over the years. Now it was his turn to do her one.

In less than fifteen minutes she had the details of what had happened in City Hall and knew Sam believed someone who worked in the building brought in the weapon, because security remembered clearing the shooter and he had definitely not been armed.

She waited for Sam to say something about Nick being in D.C. When he didn't, Fiona was very careful not to let him know she was sitting across a restaurant table from his brother-in-law. Her two evenings spent with Nick would stay her secret until she figured out what he wanted and whether anyone at all needed to know.

Chapter 4

The wedding on Saturday was lovely. The bride, who had roomed with Fiona for a couple of years when they were both starting out in Portland before moving to the East Coast for a job on Capitol Hill, looked radiant and the groom handsome. The ceremony was everything it was supposed to be—joyful, festive, celebratory.

Leaving the church, Fiona cornered Hank Lewis to continue the conversation from the evening before. He gave her a couple ideas on rocks to turn over, but eventually Fiona felt sorry for the woman he was with, who'd never even been to Portland, much less been involved in the city's local politics, and moved on.

Sitting in a coffee shop killing time between the noon wedding and the two o'clock reception, she got a text from Nick asking how the wedding had gone. He was off to the artist reception for his show opening in Alexandria himself.

Hmm, what if she went back to D.C. this afternoon instead of the next day? She could surprise Nick at the gallery. Maybe have dinner with him. She had the rest of the weekend free; he'd said he did. It was tempting.

Two evenings with him had convinced her there was something between them; something that might be worth exploring. She still wasn't sure why he had sought her out. Maybe he needed to occupy his time between assignments and she was conveniently in town. That wouldn't be all that bad, now that she thought about it. No complications. No messy emotions. Not the worst way to get back out in the world after more than a year of self-imposed isolation.

The signals were all there saying he was interested. She didn't think she was so rusty she'd misinterpreted him. She was sure by now he wasn't doing a favor for his sister. Among other reasons, wouldn't Sam have mentioned it if his wife was behind the meet-up?

And she doubted his sister would have asked him to hold her hand or put his arm around her, much less give her good-night kisses that left her breathless and wanting more. Maybe tonight…

The thought of what "more" might mean made the decision for her—if the hot, young guy was interested, so was she. She might not live a life as exciting as a world-traveling photographer but she wasn't foolish enough to walk away from the chance to spend time with someone who seemed attracted to her regardless of her travel experience. She'd put in an appearance at the reception, say hello to the bride and groom, eat wedding cake, and then head back to D.C.

The drive back to Washington gave her plenty of time to think about her impulsive decision. Halfway there she began to have serious doubts. Maybe she was kidding herself thinking he was interested. Maybe it would be better to go back to her hotel. Maybe she could get her room back a day early. An infinite loop of the reasons she shouldn't do what she was about to do ran through her head: he was a kid; he'd have other plans for the evening.

Oh, God, maybe he had a date. There was a possibility she hadn't considered.

Should she call him and see if it was okay to drop in? Just outside the city, she pulled over at a rest stop and tried calling but got his voicemail, texted him and sat watching the screen for fifteen minutes before acknowledging it was likely he wasn't paying attention to his phone.

She decided to cruise by the gallery and see if he appeared to be dateless, then make up her mind about going in. If it didn't look good, she'd head to Capitol Hill.

Arriving in Alexandria, she located the address and parked a block away. Casually strolling past the place, she glanced in, not sure what she would see or how he would react.

She needn't have worried. Nick spied her before she could get past the large front display window, broke off the conversation he was having with an older couple and came out the door.

Putting his arm around her shoulders, he kissed her. "This makes the evening even better," he said before leading her inside. His obvious pleasure calmed her last vestige of fear about his not wanting her there.

His exhibit was a series of black-and-white images he'd taken on a trip to Israel and Palestine with a peace group eighteen months before. He started to explain them to her but was interrupted by the gallery owner, who wanted him to meet a couple who'd just purchased one of the photographs.

On her own Fiona perused the exhibit. His skill and sensitivity in showing the impact of the long-running conflict on the lives of people on both sides of the issue, without advocating for either, moved her. And shooting the images as he did seemed an interesting choice for a subject so clearly not black and white. Although having once seen the photos shot that way, she couldn't imagine them otherwise.

Maybe there was more to this man—not to mention what he did for a living—than she gave him credit for. Nick's images brought her to understand the conflict on an emotional level in a way all the millions of words written about it had not.

After she looked over the exhibit, she watched him. She admired the easy manner he had with total strangers, some of whom didn't seem to know much about either the subject or the art form. She liked the way he handled the questions he was asked about his work—most of them, she noticed, repeats of the ones he'd just answered five minutes before.

At seven, the art gallery owner said, "We're done here for the evening, Nick. It seemed to go well, don't you think?"

"It did, thanks to your mailing list." He motioned to Fiona. "Adam, I'd like you to meet a friend of mine, Fiona McCarthy. Fiona, Adam Healy."

"I like your gallery, Adam," Fiona said as they shook hands.

"Thank you. And thank you for coming to Nick's reception. Now why don't the two of you go have a drink or something?"

"Any recommendations on a place to eat nearby?" Nick asked.

"Nostrano. An Italian place about two blocks away. You'll love it."

"Sound good to you, Fee?"

Fiona usually hated to have her name shortened but somehow she couldn't find it in her to complain when Nick did it. "Sounds great."

• • •

They were just about finished with their coffee and tiramisu when Nick said, "Thank you for coming back early to see my exhibit. I was surprised—and happy—to see you."

She ducked her head, not wanting to meet his eyes as she said, "Well, I didn't know many people at the reception. And your exhibit sounded so interesting when you talked about it. Besides, there were some other things I thought I could do back in the District." When she looked up, his expression was beyond sexy, the bedroom eyes with lids at half-mast, the tip of his tongue flicking over his upper lip as if lapping up the last bit of cream from a saucer.

"Oh?" he asked. "What were the other things you wanted to do? I'd be really interested in knowing." The tone of his voice was low and intimate.

"Yes, I…uh…well, there's…" She stopped, not sure how to continue the conversation, wanting to say he drew her back, not his work, but afraid to tell him in case it was a mistake.

He let the silence build for a few long moments before saying, "Maybe I can finish the sentence for you. You came back early because you feel the same electricity between us that I do, and you want to find out what we can do about it."

Gulping hard, she nodded; words still out of reach for her.

He took her hand as he continued, "And you thought since I'd told you I was free for the rest of the weekend, I might be interested in doing the same."

Another nod.

"Then why are we sitting here when I have a perfectly good apartment waiting where we can satisfy our curiosity?"

She followed him to his neighborhood, then wasted a frustrating five minutes looking for a parking place. At the point where she would have double-parked and the ticket be damned, she found a place. Nick was waiting outside his building when she finally got there, took her hand without saying another word, and together they went up the steps to his apartment. When they got inside, she could feel her heart rate kick into a gear previously unknown to her and her breathing become almost audible.

Dear God, he'd barely touched her and she was a puddle of desire.

Putting his hands on her shoulders he said, "We can go as fast or as slow as you want, Fee. I want to do what you want to do."

She answered him by bringing his mouth to hers, brushing her lips over his, back and forth, side to side, teasing, asking him for more. He pulled her into his arms and she relaxed against him, a soft moan coming from the back of her throat as he took control of the kiss. Shifting his body backward slightly, he pulled her onto her tiptoes and hard against him where she could feel his growing erection.

When he had her where he seemed to want her, he moved his hands up her back and into her hair. Without any urging from him, she parted her lips to let him in, their tongues doing a slow, sensual dance around each other. He found the place at the corners of her mouth that made her gasp and moan again, nibbled at her lower lip as though she was more dessert for him to savor.

Eventually, reluctantly, she pulled away so she could get some oxygen to her heated brain. "Should we continue this here or...?" he asked, leaving the question open and the decision to go to his bedroom to her.

Her hands flat on his chest, she smiled up at him and said, "I hear there's a big-screen TV someplace other than the living room. Why don't you show it to me?"

"I have something else in mind to show you, but we can start there," he said, taking her hand again.

He had turned toward his bedroom when she stopped him. "There's one thing you should know."

"Unless you're married to an armed and dangerous man who's found his way to the building looking for you, I can't think of anything else I need to know."

"Seriously, Nick."

He looked like he was trying to control his mouth from breaking out in a smile. "Okay. Seriously, Fee."

"It's been a very long time since...well, since the last time. I might be a big disappointment to you."

He let the smile appear. "I hear it's like riding a bike. It comes back to you very quickly. Besides, you don't kiss like someone who'll disappoint me." To prove his point, he claimed her mouth in another scorching kiss before pulling her to the bedroom.

When they got there he turned on the bedside light and waved at the TV. "There it is, a big TV as advertised, although there's nothing I want to see right now...well, nothing on television. There's my desk, which holds no interest for me either. But this," he bounced onto the bed and then up again before pulling back an indigo blue patterned quilt to reveal crisp looking white sheets,

"I am in the mood for doing something here. How about I get you comfortable so we can figure out what it is?"

She nodded agreement, afraid to speak for fear she'd be unable to form a coherent sentence. Slowly, almost reverently, he began undressing her, kissing her neck as he slipped off her jacket. Then, as he unzipped the back of her dress, he took her earlobe between his teeth and gently tugged at it before running his tongue over the ridges of her ear. Holding onto his arms for support, shivering with desire, she felt her knees begin to wobble dangerously as he blew his warm breath over her damp ear.

How—or when—he unhooked her bra, she wasn't sure but suddenly it was on the floor with her jacket and dress and she was left in her heels and panties. He lowered her onto the bed, then knelt by her to remove her shoes.

It was the sexiest thing she'd ever seen, him on his knees, his eyes hot with desire, the tip of his tongue visible as he concentrated on unbuckling and unwrapping the straps on her shoes from around her ankles. She felt like Cinderella. Except, of course, Cindy was trying the shoes on, not having them taken off. And was dressed. And anticipating sex wasn't part of it, at least not in the Disney version.

When both shoes were off, he stood up and began to undress. He held her gaze as he shed the leather vest and white shirt he wore, revealing the most beautiful chest she'd ever seen, a testament to a well-used gym membership maybe, or toting around heavy photography equipment. All she knew was she wanted to feel the hardness against her breasts and her fingers were itching to trace the valleys between those muscles.

After toeing off his shoes, his trousers and shorts were off. She wasn't surprised his abs were as impressive as his chest. Not to mention his erection. Here was yet another part of him her fingers wanted to touch.

Just before he slid under the sheet with her he opened the drawer to the bedside table and pulled out condoms. She wondered if he'd been planning this or was always prepared just in case. The thought was gone in seconds as he pulled her body against his, pressing his erection against her abdomen. They would need them. He was prepared. That's all that mattered.

As he rained kisses from her temple to the corner of her mouth and on to the hollow of her throat, she rocked her hips against his and was rewarded by a deep, guttural sound in his throat. Emboldened by the groan, she ran her hand down his abdomen, reaching for what she'd wanted to touch since she'd seen him strip off his boxers.

He stopped her hand. "As good as I know it would feel, you'd better not or I'm likely to embarrass myself and neither one of us will have a very good time." He gave her a quick kiss on the nose and a half smile as he released her hand.

She grinned at him. "Must be what I get for fooling around with a sweet young thing."

He kissed the smile away, seeming to ignore what she'd said, and moved his hand tantalizingly slowly down her belly, the feel of his mouth and his hand clouding her mind, increasing the need to have him touch her in the most sensitive place on her body, where she was aching to feel him.

And then he was there, circling her clitoris with his thumb while he gently, carefully used first one, then two fingers to massage inside her. It took very little time to bring her to the brink of exploding, her body arching against him. It took just a few more strokes of his thumb and she climaxed in an orgasm, surprising her with its speed and intensity, as well as surprising her with the skill of the man who gave it to her.

• • •

He wasn't sure he could hold on much longer, he wanted to be inside her so badly. She was everything he wanted in bed with a woman and more—sexy, responsive, passionate—and she was wet and ready for him. God knows he was ready for her. But he wanted to savor every minute of what he was sure—based on her powerful orgasm—would be mind-blowing sex with one of the most beautiful women he'd ever known. Most importantly, though, he wanted to make sure she had gotten all the pleasure he could give her this first time. He didn't want to disappoint her any more than she wanted to disappoint him.

After her orgasm he returned his attention to her mouth, her sweet, sweet mouth, nipping at her lips, licking the lusciousness of her. When he felt her press her body against his, heard the soft sounds she made at the back of her throat, he knew he wanted to hear those sounds again and again. Wanted to be the man who made her moan and ache for his kiss. Tonight. As many nights as she'd let him.

Wanted to have his mouth and his hands on her breasts where he circled first one nipple, then the other with his tongue, bringing them to hard little peaks, suckling, massaging, eliciting yet more sexy sounds from her. She shifted restlessly against him and he knew he had only a modicum of control left before he would have to be inside her; have to explode inside her.

Before he could reach for the condom, she grabbed it, tore open the packet and held it up to him, as if asking "You or me?" He pulled back and let her roll it down over his aching, throbbing penis, his control now on a ragged edge. When she was finished, she tugged at him until he was back between her legs. Slowly he entered her, feeling her tight, hot core stretch, expand to accommodate him, then close around him so they fit together.

Kissing his way up her chest to her mouth, he used his tongue to taste her again. And again. And again.

It didn't take long for her to climax a second time. This time, he followed.

They lay tangled together as he tried to bring his breathing back to something close to normal. Eventually, he had to leave to get rid of the condom but on his return, he pulled her into his arms and said, "Okay, 'sweet young thing.' What the hell was that about?"

She took his hand and kissed it but didn't meet his gaze. "I shouldn't have said it. I'm sorry. But I know you're a lot younger than I am. I got carried away. I guess I'm enjoying some sort of fantasy thing."

"I appreciate being your fantasy, but why do you think you're so much older than I am?"

"I know how old Amanda is and she's always said you were her baby brother, by a lot of years. So I'm guessing maybe you're twenty-two, twenty-three. Much younger than I am."

"So, you think I'm only a year or so past my last outbreak of acne and you're an ancient old lady who's, what, my grandmother's age?"

Suppressing a smile, she shook her head. "No, not really, I'm thirty-two."

"I majored in journalism, not math, but even so, I'll be twenty-eight next month, which, if my math is correct, means you're only four years older than I am. Amanda exaggerates so she can boss me around."

"You've made me feel less like I'm robbing the cradle. Thanks."

He untangled his legs from hers and backed far enough away to give him the space to look directly in her eyes. "Even if I were as young as you thought, what's the big deal? It's nothing more than a number." He traced her mouth with his forefinger again. "Just a number, Fee." She sucked on his finger, kissed the inside of his wrist. He ducked his head and returned to her breasts, tugging gently at her nipples with his teeth and lips, pulling them, one at a time, into erect points. "All that matters is this."

"Oh, Nick." She groaned.

"You like that? How about this?" He moved down her body, kissing his way around her navel until he reached her sex. She raised her hips to him so he could make love to her with his mouth, flicking his tongue across the spot between her legs where all her attention was concentrated.

When she moaned and gasped, he kissed his way back up her body and turned her onto her side, facing him. He pulled her leg up over his hip so he was nudging against her sex. He was already hard again and he had another condom ready to put on.

"Oh, my," she murmured. "You're..."

"Not a sweet young thing, but I'm not old either." With his mouth on hers and his hands everywhere on her body he wanted to go, she was better than any fantasy he'd had about what it would be like. And he loved it.

He took his time, paying slow and careful attention to her mouth and her breasts, her arms, every inch of her body, bringing her along, stopping to kiss her, to nibble at her neck. When he thought she could bear it no longer, he put on the condom, brought her leg up higher to hook onto his back and with one thrust was deep inside her.

He tipped up her chin, then touched her eyes, one at a time. "Look at me, Fiona," he whispered. "I want to see your eyes when you come this time."

She opened her eyes and he saw.

Afterward, he thought she'd dozed off so he slowly, carefully edged away from her, intending to head for the bathroom again. But she wasn't really asleep. She started, her eyes flying open, looking surprised. She ran her hand lightly down his back and said, "Is everything okay?"

"Everything's fine. I was looking to see if there was another condom out because, you know, since you're messing around with a sweet young thing, we might need it."

"If I officially apologize, will you forget what I said?"

He laughed and drew her into his arms. "I'm never letting you forget."

"If we put the condom to use in the next half hour, will you at least not mention it again tonight?"

"Yes, if you'll put the shades up on your eyes. A little while ago, I saw a woman I want to see again. She was willing to be vulnerable, she's passionate…"

Fiona put her hand over his mouth and didn't say anything. What he saw on her face said she was as overwhelmed by what he said as by the physical sensations they'd both just experienced. Maybe even, he thought, overwhelmed enough to be afraid.

Trying to comfort her, he kissed her fingers and took her hand from his lips. "Fiona, I…"

"Sh-sh-sh. Don't say it."

"How do you know what I'm going to say?"

"We both know what you're going to say. It's what men say to women when they've just had sex with them. Don't insult me. Just leave it the way it is. No expectations. No demands. Not from me. I've been there and done that and I don't need any more T-shirts from the experience."

"I think you're wrong. And am I so easy to brush off?"

"I can't imagine any woman brushing you off, me included. I'm just…well, just letting you know you don't have to play the game with me, I guess." She nestled into his arms. "Can we talk in the morning? I think this conversation would be better in the daylight and out of bed."

Chapter 5

She woke with a start, her face pressed into a pillow with an unfamiliar smell. Where…?

Then she remembered.

She was in Nick's bed. Where she'd spent the night. A night full of the best sex she'd ever had with a man who knew exactly what to do with his mouth, his hands, and every other pertinent part of his body. Dear God, he was good.

But now, like the worst cliché, in the full daylight of the morning after, she was wondering if she'd made the biggest mistake of her life. So, he was only a few years younger than she was. There were other complications. He lived three thousand miles away from Portland—when he was in country, which wasn't very often. He had an ego she realized—now that she'd seen more of his work—he was apparently entitled to but which was capable of swamping her, she was sure. And he was still her friend's brother. How do you have a roll in the hay with your friend's baby brother and face her when you get home? What the hell had she been thinking?

She pushed the covers back and sat up, trying to be as careful as possible so she didn't wake him. Maybe she could just sneak out, leave him a note or something, return to her hotel, think about it when the temptation to put her arms around him and hold him wasn't so close.

"Good morning, beautiful. Did you sleep well?" Nick ran his hand down her back.

Okay, so sneaking away wasn't going to work. "I did. You have a comfortable bed."

He touched the small of her back. "How did I miss this last night? You have a Celtic cross tattoo."

Grateful for the change of subject, she said, "I was in a bad place awhile back and decided I needed to do something outrageous. A tattoo may not have been the best choice, but it was better than the other things I considered—entering a convent, extended drug use, changing my name, leaving the country."

"I like it."

"Thanks. It's my private little rebellion. No one else knows it's there."

He raised an eyebrow. "Really? Is there a reason you've kept it secret?"

"I'm sure there is but not one I've given much thought to."

He pulled her back into bed. "So, you and your secret tattoo slept well?"

"We did."

"Right. Because of my comfortable mattress." He was grinning at her.

The blush she could feel flushing over her face and neck made it impossible to lie. "Well, your bed was part of the reason."

Lacing his fingers through hers, he began to tug her closer to him, kissing up her arm between words. "How about we replay some of the other parts of the reason?"

She shook off his hand. "I think I should go to my hotel, Nick. You must have things you need to do today."

"You know I have the weekend free. And you can't check into your hotel until four." He frowned at her, seriously, this time. "Are you okay? Did I do something wrong? Or was it not good for you last night?"

"Oh, dear God, no. Last night was wonderful. It was…I don't even know a word good enough to describe it. But I'm not sure we should make too much out of one night."

"How 'bout we extend the night we're not making too much out of to a night and a whole Sunday? Stay and have breakfast—in a while—and then spend the day with me. We can, I don't know, go someplace you haven't been in Washington. One of the Smithsonians. The zoo. Go look at the Constitution. Or how about The Spy Museum? The Freer? The Corcoran? The Sackler?"

By the time he got through his list, she was laughing. "Okay, one more day. And how about the Newseum? I haven't been there in forever."

"Might have guessed it would be your choice. But first things first." He wouldn't let her avoid his arms and his mouth this time, but then she didn't really try.

• • •

On the plane ride home three days later she tried to work out if her time with Nick was just a vacation thing or something else. In addition to the two dinners they'd had before she went to the wedding and the weekend they'd mostly spent together, they'd seen each other every day until the morning she left. They'd found a thousand things to talk about—family, politics, books, movies, plays, art, the world—and the sex had been amazing. But she had absolutely no idea what it meant. Maybe it was, on her part, merely a need to be held after almost two years of self-inflicted solitude and on his, a willingness to be the one who held her. She didn't know.

She'd play it by ear. Or forget about it. Which, given how much she'd enjoyed being with him both in and out of bed, seemed difficult to imagine doing. But she could try. She'd just settle back into her normal life and see what happened.

Oh, and she'd avoid any conversation with her friend Amanda in which the words "sex" and "baby brother" appeared.

• • •

Fiona lived in St. Johns, a neighborhood north of downtown Portland where the graceful St. Johns Bridge crossed the

Willamette River. Local legend, which she'd learned long ago wasn't true, claimed the cable suspension bridge, the longest of its kind in the world when it was built, had been the prototype for the Golden Gate Bridge in San Francisco. No matter how often the legend was debunked, Oregonians persisted in spreading the rumor. Mostly, Fiona believed, to annoy San Franciscans.

The St. Johns Bridge story was part of a two-pronged attack on Baghdad by the Bay. The other prong involved the original plat map for the city. It had been filed in what was then the appropriate territorial office—Oregon City, Oregon—where it remained to this day, in spite of San Francisco's best efforts to get it back. It was like the Greeks trying to get the Elgin Marbles back from the British Museum but on a much smaller scale.

The cozy Craftsman-style house where Fiona had lived for nine years had been lovingly restored by her landlord. Hardwood floors had been refinished and the built-in bookcases, sideboard, and china cabinet for which the homes were known polished to a high shine. The original stained glass panels over the windows in the dining room and entryway, having been cleaned and restored, glowed when the sun was right.

Over the years, Fiona had acquired a few pieces of reproduction Stickley furniture to go with the style of the house. Her living room had a couch, a rocker, and a leather lounge chair in the distinctive style as well as a coffee table. A set of not so distinctively styled shelves held her prized collection of vinyl records and a turntable. In her dining room was a table and chairs for six, in the kitchen, a small breakfast table and two chairs. She slept in one of the two bedrooms and used the other as a guest room and home office after losing her roommate to the nation's capital. Actually, it was less a home office than it was a refuge for Pulitzer, her orange marmalade cat.

She loved the house, loved her neighborhood, loved everything about her life. Except, of course, when she couldn't get a handle on a story she was chasing. Which was where she was on the white power story; she told her managing news editor, Ben Stern, when she got back to her desk after her trip.

He commiserated with her but said she needed to let it go for the moment and get the piece on the Anderbock bill written and then finish a piece on earthquakes she'd started researching before she left, because it had been moved up as the cover story for next week.

He also asked her to look into a new non-profit foundation. The Green Machine—an over-cutesy name she thought—financed by Duke Wellington and Sherman Bischler, purported to provide seed money for start-up businesses in the field of green energy. Her boss wanted to know if there was a connection—or a contradiction—between the foundation and the Anderbock bill.

Secretly delighted because interviewing the two men might give her a way to keep her investigation into the white power story going, she made the calls to ask for interviews with them.

Text messages from Nick continued for a few days after she returned to Portland, then stopped. No surprise, really. She knew he was on another assignment and assumed their time in Washington together was a vacation fling to him, nothing more. After all, she'd decided that's what it was. Why wouldn't he? If she just remembered to think of it that way, it would be better for all concerned.

However, he must have told his sister they'd seen each other in D.C. because the phone call he'd assured her would come finally did. And as part of her determination to consider it a fling that had been flung, Fiona blithely described the week she'd spent in Nick St. Claire's arms—in his bed—as merely a couple dinners out and a chance to see his exhibit. Amanda sounded disappointed; Fiona was almost sorry. The whole story was much more interesting.

But her time with Nick soon took a backseat to her work when, a week after she returned from D.C., Fiona snagged interviews with both Duke Wellington and Sherman Bischler.

Wellington was first. She'd never been in his office but had heard rumors of its opulence—antique Persian rugs, an extensive art collection by local artists Mel Katz, Mark Rothko, and Ray Atkeson, a view of the city—and was almost as curious about the office as she was about the man.

She dressed carefully in her most conservative suit and found herself at his door twenty minutes early for her appointment. Duke Wellington's secretary, a middle-aged woman who acted like she was guarding Fort Knox, had looked dubiously at her computer when Fiona announced she had an appointment for an interview before disappearing into his office to see if he was ready.

While she waited for the secretary's return, Fiona looked at the photos on the wall. Most prominent were two photographs of the anglophile Wellington in formal dress, being presented to Queen Elizabeth at a garden party by his friend, Nigel Hetherington, the British consul in Portland. The rest of the wall was covered by shots of Wellington with former mayors, governors, Congressmen, and senators—a preponderance of them Republicans with a few Democrats scattered in.

"Interested in my wall, are you, Ms. McCarthy?" She wasn't sure how long Duke Wellington had been standing behind her, so absorbed in the images she'd become.

"It's an impressive collection of photos, Mr. Wellington. If you ever want to write a book on Oregon politics, it looks like you have the material to do it." She turned and put her hand out for him to shake. "And it's Fiona."

"Nice to meet you. I'm Duke. I've thought about writing a book but never seem to have the time to get going on it. Maybe I could persuade you to write it for me." He waved at the open door to his office. "Come in, please. Would you like coffee? And how do you like it?"

"Thank you. Black, please." She followed him into a well-appointed space overlooking the city. The paintings she'd heard about were prominently displayed. In addition, he had several sculptures and, on well-lighted shelves, two pieces of what she recognized as Amanda St. Claire's glass art. A large, completely neat and organized desk with a Herman Miller Aeron chair behind it took pride of place in the center of the room, but Wellington waved her to a circle of leather chairs around a glass-topped table near one of the windows.

The coffee was served in matching china cups she was tempted to turn over to confirm they were English bone china. After a few sips, Wellington asked, "Now, why is *Willamette Week* interested in our little foundation?"

"We're always interested in new approaches to finding solutions to old problems, and this sounds like it fits. Do you mind if I record our interview as well as take notes?"

He shook his head; she pulled a recorder, pad, and pen out of her bag and started the interview.

Wellington explained how his interest in power generation had led to the formation of a foundation to funnel money to start-up businesses in green energy sources. The Northwest was running out of the cheap hydropower the region had grown on, and replacement sources, as well as the businesses manufacturing the elements to produce the power, were needed.

He displayed a calm and approachable demeanor during the whole interview. His delivery was smooth, he sounded convincing in his facts. His body language; leaning forward, looking directly at her, seemed to say he was as enthusiastic about this as he'd ever been about anything he'd done. He was sharp, slick, and didn't miss a trick, including the way her skirt rode up when she leaned forward to check on her recorder.

Yet it all sounded too pat; too canned. Of course, it was possible he'd given the speech too many times to too many other people. And she knew he had a reputation for disliking the press so this might be his way of protecting himself. But from what?

What could hide behind a foundation with money to loan out to green energy sources? As it was his fortune he was investing, she was sure he wasn't wasting it. He had ridden out any number of regional recessions, surviving both the timber industry going over a cliff and hi-tech taking a bath, coming out the other side in every instance with more, not less, money.

She didn't interrupt his polished flow of words until he was finished, and then she asked how these efforts fit with the Anderbock bill, which he supported, for example. He wasn't the least bit ruffled by the question, as if he'd been waiting for it. He explained how the projects they were financing would take a while to get up and running and in the meantime, coal and natural gas—which industry already knew how to use—would be needed.

After an hour she left, disappointed it had been bland, boring, and without one break in the flow of conversation to get in a question about the White Knights, however obliquely.

Two days later it was Sherman Bischler's turn. The interview felt like déjà vu, from the first moment she entered his office. It, too, was imposing with the requisite photos on the wall of the man with important people, although Bischler's were all businessmen. And his collection of artwork from local artists didn't include any work by Amanda St. Claire. He did have a large sculpture of a very fierce looking eagle. And he had flags in the office, one the Stars and Stripes, the other the Oregon state flag. The view from his office was as impressive, the furniture as expensive, the coffee as good as she'd experienced in Duke Wellington's office. Even the answers to her questions were similar.

Only the conversation after her allotted hour was different.

As Bischler walked her to the outer door of his office, he said, "I care very much about what happens in Portland; in Oregon. That's why I've put my money into this foundation. I may not be Bill Gates, but I still think I can do some good."

"It sounds like you're doing more than most. The Foundation seems like a worthwhile endeavor."

"I hope it is." He paused at the door, not opening it for her. "Given what's happening here right now, this may not be the best way to help, but it's what I can do. For the moment."

"What do you mean, what's happening?"

"The way things are being run in Portland right now creates a bad business climate."

"Can you give me an example?"

"When have we ever had an attempt on a mayor's life? And surely you've heard the other rumors."

"Rumors? I'm not sure what you mean." *Where the hell was he going with this?* She broke eye contact with him, glancing down at the pen she still held in her hand, looking for something to write on.

"I think you do." His voice was low, as if sharing a great confidence. "You're a smart woman. But if the rumors are true, a smart woman would be a careful woman."

She felt her breath catch and her eyes widen. "Are you giving me some kind of warning?"

"Now how could I be warning anyone when I don't know any more than you do about the rumors running around? No, I'm just saying, it's not, shall we say, stable in Portland at the moment. The atmosphere's not good for business and it's not good for crusading reporters."

The smile she tried to get out wouldn't budge. "Thanks. I'll keep what you said in mind." Reaching for the doorknob she let herself out. Later, in the elevator, as she frantically scribbled the conversation down in her notebook, she thought, *Ben is not fucking going to believe this.*

Chapter 6

The third phone caller in less than ten minutes got the brunt of her annoyance at the repeated interruptions. "Fiona McCarthy," she snapped, warning whoever had dared to contact her to make it short.

"Oops. Sounds like I'm interrupting."

She relaxed back in her chair and smiled into the phone. "You're not, Nick. Everyone else is. The phone won't stop today. How are you?"

"Surprised you're willing to talk to me. I'm sorry I haven't been in touch. We've been so far out in the wilderness there was no signal. It's hard to believe how many places there are in North America where you can't make a cell phone call or get wifi. At least no one was shooting at me there, which was a pleasant change."

"No apology needed." She felt a tap on her shoulder. "Hold on a minute, will you?" She put her phone down to look over a piece of copy a colleague had thrust in front of her, talked over a couple of changes with him, then went back to the phone call. "Sorry, where were we?"

"I was interrupting you at work."

"It's Monday, when we start to put the paper to bed. This week is particularly bad for me because I've got the cover story."

"So, I guess you're not free for dinner tonight."

"You're in Portland? Great. But yes...I mean, no...well, whichever answer means I can't have dinner with you tonight. I'll be here until nine or ten."

"Buy you a drink after you're finished?"

"A quick one. Are you staying at Sam and Amanda's?"

"No, at the Paramount Hotel."

For two seconds she wondered about the significance of his staying at a hotel, but then the thought was gone. "I'll meet you in the bar there. I'll call you when I leave the office."

At nine forty-five she walked into the bar, sure she must look like the survivor of the kind of natural disaster she'd been writing about. Her navy blue linen pants were wrinkled, her white scoop-neck knit top had printer ink on one sleeve, and her eyes looked like they'd packed bags for a 'round-the-world cruise. She'd run a brush through her shoulder-length hair and applied fresh lipstick before she got out of the car without even looking in a mirror, sure if she saw how dragged-from-the-rubble she looked, she'd cancel the drink date until she could get a good night's sleep and a change of clothes.

As she approached the booth where he was waiting, Nick stood, reaching out his hand to her and saying, "Hello, beautiful" before holding her a bit longer than polite convention demanded as he kissed her cheek. She slid into the booth; he sat close beside her, keeping her hand.

"Sorry I'm such a disheveled welcoming committee, but it's been a long day," she said.

"You look great even with ink decorating your chin."

Her hand wiped automatically at her face but came away with no ink to show she'd gotten rid of the offending substance. "Oh, hell. My printer ran out of ink at a bad moment and I made a mess of changing the cartridge because I was in a hurry. I'll go get it off as soon as I order a beer."

He dipped a cocktail napkin into his glass of water and, holding her face in one hand, rubbed at the spot. "There. Your face is ink-free and as beautiful as always."

She smiled and ducked her head at the compliment, then ordered a glass of local microbrew from the server, after which she sighed and sank back into the booth. "Every Monday I wonder what it would be like to have a job where we don't start the week in a frenzy. Unfortunately, I love where I work so I guess I'll never find out."

"So what's your cover story this week? Or is it so secret you'd have to kill me if you told me?"

"This one doesn't come close to being worth killing for. The story is about the earthquake danger in Portland and the Northwest coast."

"You're kidding."

"No, it's serious stuff. Apparently we're overdue for a specific kind of very destructive earthquake. It's called a…"

"…subduction zone earthquake. A more powerful kind than the slip-strike earthquakes they have on the San Andreas fault."

"I'm impressed."

"Don't be. One of the stories I came to do photographs on is about earthquakes. When I asked if you were kidding, I meant it was weird we're working on related stories."

"I thought you said you were coming here on a tourism story." He was watching her with such a warm, affectionate look, she sat up straighter and pushed her hair back from her face to try and improve the view for him.

"Both, actually. The one I talked about in D.C. is a story my friend Travis pitched to a travel magazine. He started out featuring one or two of the Cascade mountains, Hood and St. Helens, if I remember right. Then he added Mt. Adams and Jefferson. I'm afraid to read his texts any more for fear he's added more. The earthquake one is for *National Geographic*. It shouldn't take much time. The other could be a longer assignment."

"Is the earthquake story only about Portland?"

"No, it's a major cover story on the earthquake risks in the United States in places other than California, which everyone knows about. The Northwest is only part of the story. I took it because I would be here anyway."

"And the other…you said it was a friend."

"Yeah, a writer friend has been bugging me to do this with him. I put him off for a while but finally agreed because I like him and so I'd have an excuse to come to Portland. He'll be here in a week or so. I'll do some scouting shots for him until he arrives so he can decide what he wants to include."

"I'm always envious of the time magazine writers seem to have to figure out what to write. The cover this week? It was so interesting I could have spent months researching it. But I only got a few weeks."

"You're spending more than a few weeks on the story you were talking about in Washington, aren't you?"

"Only because I can't get anything nailed down."

"Still smoke and mirrors?"

"Still."

They talked for a half hour until she finished her beer. "I better get home."

"No chance you'd…" He didn't finish the sentence but from the look in his eyes she knew what he was asking.

She shook her head. "Tomorrow and the rest of what we have to do to get the paper out will arrive at all too early an hour."

He settled the bill with the server and they walked to the lobby of the hotel. "How about dinner tomorrow night?"

"Tomorrow's great."

"What's your favorite restaurant?"

"Higgins."

"Higgins, it is. Will seven-thirty work?"

"Make it eight, just in case I have some last minute stuff on my story."

"I'll make reservations and meet you there." He put his hands on her shoulders and kissed her, stopping just before she ran out of breath and the will to leave. "I'll see you tomorrow night, then."

She started toward the revolving door then stopped and called to his retreating back. "Nick?"

"Yes?" He turned as he answered her.

"I'm glad you're here."

• • •

In the elevator going up to his floor, Nick consoled himself with knowing Fiona had been glad to see him, had squeezed in a drink around what was clearly a hectic schedule, and had agreed to dinner the next night even if she hadn't been eager to jump into his bed, which is what he'd have preferred. But he was happy with what he got—another chance the next night.

Ever since the week she'd spent in Washington, he'd been obsessed with getting to see her again. He couldn't remember the last time he'd been this intrigued by a woman. Maybe it was because he could sense she was holding something back, in spite of the amazing time they'd had in D.C. He didn't know what it could be, but he sure as hell wanted to find out.

Which was why he wasn't staying with Amanda. With a meddling sister, his brother-in-law the cop, and his nosy four-year-old niece, the idea of getting to know more about Fiona while he was staying there was laughable. Not to mention he'd have a hard time convincing her to let him sneak her in and out of the guest room.

Amanda had sounded disappointed when he'd told her he wouldn't be staying with them. When he explained his writer expected him to be downtown and accessible, she reluctantly accepted the idea. He hadn't told her the writer wouldn't be in town for a week.

Nor had he told her how he got the assignment. Hell, he hadn't told Fiona the whole story. He'd turned down the job of photographing in the Cascades for a better paying gig in Belize. He'd referred his friend Travis to another photographer. But after his time with Fiona he'd called Travis and told him he'd changed his mind.

Once he convinced Travis he needed to go to Portland, he had to find a gig for the photographer Travis had hired in his place, get out of the assignment in Belize without pissing off a favorite client and move up the timing for the earthquake shoot. All for the chance to pursue Fiona to Portland. Seeing her tonight, ink on her face and everything, convinced him all the work was worth it. He'd been to Belize. She was way more interesting.

Chapter 7

Not wanting to look like she'd been the victim of a natural disaster when she saw Nick again, Fiona took a change of clothes to work the next day. When she'd donned the dress, slipped on the heels, refreshed her makeup, and fluffed her hair, the "wow" she got from her boss gave her some confidence the dark teal green pencil dress and matching shrug had been a good choice.

Nick's reaction confirmed it. He was waiting inside the door at Higgins when she arrived and the look in his eyes as he kissed her could have peeled the paint off the walls. The host was impressed, although at a somewhat less heated level. Before Nick could identify himself and the time of their reservation, the man behind the desk said, "Fiona! You look great! Where've you been? We've missed you."

"Hi, Jim. Thanks. I've been slammed. I was back East, then chasing a story here." She turned to her date. "This is Nick St. Claire, Amanda's brother. He's a photojournalist in town on assignment. Be nice to him, will you?"

"Of course we will. I wondered if you were related to Amanda when I saw your name. And if you'd told us who you were with, Mr. St. Claire, we'd have known where to seat you. Luckily, Fiona's favorite table's free."

Nick laughed. "Believe me, if I'd known throwing around the names of my sister and my date would get me a good table, I'd have told you."

"Welcome to Oregon, Nick," Fiona said as she followed the host, "where the whole state's a small town. Not everyone likes being only three degrees separated from everyone else but I love it." *Love it? She wouldn't have it any other way.*

Jim seated them at a table in the lower level by the window where it was quiet; almost secluded. When their server came to take drink orders she asked if Fiona was having her usual. She nodded. Nick said, "I'll have the same."

"You're very trusting," Fiona said when the server left. "Suppose it's some sort of frou frou girly drink."

"First, you never ordered one when we were in D.C. And second, the fact you'd call it a frou frou girly drink shows my confidence isn't misplaced."

"I hope you like Maker's Mark Manhattans straight up."

"My favorite bourbon." He closed the menu. "And since you seem to be on a roll, why don't you order for both of us."

Not sure what to make of it, she took a moment before replying, finally going with, "You're an interesting man, Nick St. Claire."

"I'm trying to be."

"Really? How come?"

"I shouldn't think it would take an investigative reporter to figure it out." His smile was slow in appearing but seductive when it showed up.

She cocked her head and stared at him again, trying to read in his hazel eyes what he meant, not sure she was ready for what she saw. Finally she dropped her gaze and opened her menu. "Everything here is good. Greg Higgins, the owner, was one of the first people in the region to go locavore."

He let her diversionary tactic hang for a moment before saying, "I always think that word sounds funny. If an herbivore eats vegetables and a carnivore eats meat, it follows a locavore should eat the natives, doesn't it?"

"You've met some strange people in your travels. Or have you've eaten some strange food?" She went back to perusing the menu. "I think I'll pick out dinner without following either of those trains of thought." Ignoring Nick's laugh she went on. "Greg's loyalty to local growers is one of the reasons I like this place. The other, of course, is I like what they do with the ingredients."

Their server returned with their Manhattans and recited the specials. When she left, Fiona raised her glass and said, "Here's to a successful visit."

Nick clinked glasses with her. "Thank you. I hope I get what I came for, too."

He probably meant his photographs but Fiona couldn't help wondering—and hoping—it wasn't all he meant.

When the server came back for their order, Nick handed her his menu and said, "Ms. McCarthy is ordering for both of us." Fiona smiled and said, "We'll split the spring greens and hazelnut salad to start and have the duck on the menu and the halibut special."

The order taken care of, their menus and the server disappeared. "Dinner sounds great," Nick said. "But I was surprised there was no salmon on offer."

"I think we're between seasons—too late for one run, too early for another. My favorite is Copper River salmon, but the season's still about a month or so away." She handed the wine list to him. "Here, I left the hard part for you—picking out a wine to go with both duck and halibut."

Nick motioned to their server and, when she got there, engaged in a long discussion about wines culminating in the selection of an Oregon Pinot Noir.

They had just settled back with their drinks again when there was yet another interruption, this time from Duke Wellington. He approached the table, his hand out to Fiona. "I thought that was you. With your red hair, you can't hide very well, can you?" he said as they shook hands. "How's your story on our little foundation coming? Can we expect to be inundated with calls from admirers of your prose any time soon?"

"It's coming along just fine, thanks. Not sure when we plan to run it, but I'll let you know when it does." She indicated her date. "Duke, this is Nick St. Claire. He's a photojournalist here on assignment. Nick, meet Duke Wellington. He's started a very interesting foundation funding green energy start-ups."

"Nice to meet you," Wellington said. Nick had stood and the two men shook hands. "St. Claire. I don't suppose you're related to our Amanda St. Claire, are you?"

"I am. She's my sister."

"I have two pieces of her work. If your photographic images are as good as her glass, your parents raised two remarkable artists."

"Thank you. They would be pleased with the compliment."

"Well, I don't want to interrupt you two anymore than I already have. I was just on my way out and wanted to let Fiona know I'd seen her. Nice to meet you, Nick. See you again, Fiona, I'm sure."

What the hell did that mean; he wanted to let me know he'd seen me? And I'm not able to hide? How creepy was that?

Watching him leave, Nick had a puzzled expression on his face. He stared after Duke Wellington for a few moments before taking his seat again. "Why do I get an uneasy feeling about him?"

"You, too? I had a similar feeling when I interviewed him recently, but I can't put my finger on why."

"There's just something off about him, like he's putting on an act."

"Maybe it's knowing he's one of the guys I've been hearing is behind what I'm digging into that's tainting my opinion of him. Or maybe it's just his well-known dislike of the press. I don't know."

The salad arrived as she was finishing up her musings and Duke Wellington disappeared from their conversation.

They'd finished their salad and were talking, Nick with his hand over hers, when two couples followed the host down the short flight of steps to their part of the restaurant. The first couple consisted of a tall, handsome, dark-haired man, his hand at the small of the back of an equally dark-haired woman not much shorter in her heels than he was. Both were in their thirties and dressed in business clothes.

The second couple looked more casual. The man wore dark denim jeans and cowboy boots with a tan jacket and a white dress shirt and had his arm around the shoulders of a woman in a short, flippy skirt and a lace-edged blouse. Her impossibly high platform sandals looked like an attempt to make her five-foot-nothing self get a bit closer to the height of the man she was with.

Fiona quickly moved her hand from under Nick's and waved at Margo Keyes and her husband, Tony Alessandro. Nick stood up to kiss his sister, Amanda, and say hello to her husband, Sam Richardson.

"So this is the previous engagement keeping you from having dinner with us, is it, Nicky?" Amanda said as she hugged her brother. She bent and kissed Fiona. "And you, my friend, have been keeping things from me, haven't you?"

Fiona was happy when Margo interjected, "What're you two doing here?"

"Duh. Eating dinner. And how'd you both do in court today?" Fiona replied.

"How'd you know we were in court today?"

"Your hair is up in a twist and you're both in very nice looking suits. Court's the only place anyone dresses up for any more," Fiona said.

"Very observant. And correct. Tony had his first outing in a Multnomah County court as the arresting officer. I won the case I was prosecuting, which prominently featured the testimony of one Detective Sam Richardson who, in spite of the fact he defies your stereotype about dressing up for court, was very persuasive with my jury. So, when he told me he and Amanda were celebrating, we decided to tag along."

"Celebrating the triumph of justice over evil-doers are you, Sam?" Nick asked.

"We're not celebrating my accomplishments tonight, as impressive as they are. We're celebrating your sister's. She's just signed with a gallery in New York and she'll be having a solo show there," Sam said.

"Awesome, Amanda" Nick said, kissing his sister again. "How come you didn't tell me about it when we talked?"

"I just got it firmed up today. I tried to get hold of you this afternoon to tell you and see if your 'previous engagement' was still on, but I couldn't reach you. Were you out shooting without your phone?" Amanda said.

"I was at Mt. St. Helens. Had a phone but no reception in spots. And, to be honest, I was in a hurry when I got back and didn't check for messages."

"No cell coverage? That's not good, Nicky. Were you alone? You shouldn't go places alone if you can't be sure you'll have cell phone coverage."

"Did you know there was no reception at all when I was in the Amazon six months ago?"

"No, I didn't, but I don't live in the Amazon and wouldn't have Mom on my back if something happened to you. She'd be after some magazine, not me. You really shouldn't be out there alone."

"Amanda," her husband interrupted, "maybe you could have this conversation with your brother when he doesn't have a dinner companion with him. What do you think?"

"Thanks, Sam. I appreciate the help," Nick said. "A lecture from my sister on looking both ways before I cross the street doesn't exactly put me in the best light when I'm trying to impress a woman."

"Sorry, Fiona, I'm behaving like..." Amanda started.

"Like she usually does, if you want to know the truth, Fee," Nick finished.

"He's right, Fiona. His older sister and mine spend too much time intruding into their brothers' lives and making damn nuisances of themselves. Right, Nick?" Sam asked.

"I wouldn't think of contradicting my older and much wiser brother-in-law."

"I don't intrude, Nicky, I'm just concerned," Amanda said.

By this time the host had become impatient waiting at the table for the foursome. Nick said, "How about we continue talking after dinner? I'll treat for dessert and a nightcap to celebrate and to make amends for trying to earn a living when my interfering sister wanted to talk to me."

"Great," Sam said. "Grab a table in the bar here, if you can, and we'll join you when we're finished. If you can't get a table, we can go down the street to the Heathman."

"Since my date has an in with the management, we'll let Fiona get us a table. Champagne, Amanda, or something else?"

"Oh, definitely champagne," she said. "I think being in a gallery in New York is worth champagne. Especially if you're buying."

A little over an hour later, the six of them were at a table in the bar where, thanks to Fiona's intervention, there was a "reserved" sign and a bottle of chilled Veuve Cliquot waiting for them. Nick arranged with their server to get the bill, then returned to the table where he settled next to Fiona and draped his arm proprietarily around the back of her chair.

When they'd ordered desserts, poured the champagne, and made a toast, Fiona said, "This is so exciting, Amanda. How'd it happen?"

"The gallery owner saw my work last fall in Seattle and contacted me. Everything is all signed and I may have a show there as early as this winter."

"Mom will be all over this," Nick said. "She's already been to D.C. to see my exhibit, accompanied by friends she'd dragged in from the surrounding states. For New York, she'll set up base camp someplace in the city and bring in the whole Eastern seaboard."

"When I called to tell her about it I swear I could hear her clicking keys on her laptop. If she wasn't checking out some ultrasound images she was probably researching hotels close to the gallery," Amanda said.

"The good news is her friends bought some of my work. You'll probably have the same thing happen." He turned to Fiona. "Have you ever met our parents, Fee?"

"For a few minutes at Sam and Amanda's wedding. Not to talk to."

"Conversations with our mother are an interesting cultural experience. Like being examined in an adolescent rite of passage in a tribal society someplace."

"It sounds like I need to be on assignment far, far away when they come to town," Fiona said.

"Sorry, the out-of-town-excuse is exclusively mine," Nick said, hugging her. "You'll have to find another."

"Fiona, don't let them scare you. Dr. and Mr. St. Claire are really nice people," Sam said.

"Of course you think they're nice. My mom adored you before she even met you." Amanda said.

"I met her by e-mail first. I'm more impressive in writing, apparently," Sam said.

"Your mom is obviously a doctor, Amanda, what's your dad do?" Tony asked.

"Mom's an OB-GYN. Since he retired from business, Dad runs the family trust."

"How come I didn't know you two had a family trust?" Fiona said, looking first at her friend then at her date.

"Our great-grandfather on the St. Claire side set up a trust to hold real estate and pay for college. On my mother's side, we had a stockbroker grandfather who set up trusts for us to inherit when we turned twenty-five. All very weird and nineteenth century," Amanda said.

"But when you marry into it," Sam said, leaning over and kissing his wife on the temple, "and gain not only a talented and beautiful wife who loves you but who already owns a home in Alameda and a beach house, it's not bad."

Chapter 8

After the dessert party broke up, Fiona and Nick walked through the Park Blocks toward his hotel. It was a pleasant spring evening and, in a move that reminded her of their walk around the Tidal Basin in Washington, Nick took her hand as they strolled unhurriedly between the beds of red and yellow tulips in full bloom.

"So, a trust fund baby," Fiona said. "Must be nice. What's it like?" *Crap. That sounded bad as soon as it left her mouth. What was it about this man that made her forget how to filter her words?*

"The good thing was we could go to any college where we were accepted and had an income when we graduated, so we could get established in careers that aren't always easy to start in without a safety net. The bad part is the tone in people's voice when they say 'trust fund baby.'"

She dipped her head and said, "I'm sorry. I didn't mean to sound insulting. It's just so far outside my experience, I'm not sure how to process it."

"It's okay. You're not alone. It's why I don't talk about it. Amanda's more comfortable with it, I guess. At least she makes jokes about having robber baron ancestors whose wise investments gave us a nice life."

"You shouldn't be embarrassed. Look at what the two of you have done with your lives. It's not as if you've been sitting around eating bon-bons and having your nails done."

"Maybe. Although sometimes I think the reason I like challenging assignments is because it makes me feel like I'm paying my dues for the good luck of being born into my family."

"I begin to see why your sister hovers. You take many chances with your work?"

"Not really. Are you worried?" He put his arm around her shoulder and squeezed her in an affectionate hug.

She slipped her arm around his waist and decided to change the subject rather than answer the question. "So, where did you go to college?"

He had an amused expression on his face as if her evasion of his question was what he expected. "Columbia."

"Good journalism school."

"Exactly. The j-school and the chance to live in New York for a few years were the attractions. Where did you go to school?"

"Washington State University, in Pullman, which is so far east in Washington State it practically qualifies as Idaho. I was a communications major with journalism as my minor."

"And what's your family like?"

"As different from yours as it's possible to be. My father was a longshoreman at the Port of Tacoma and my mother was an office manager for a local real estate developer. You ever been to Tacoma?"

"Yup. One summer while I was in college, I interned with a photojournalist and we covered a strike at the port. You didn't want to go back when you graduated?"

"I thought about it, but the job offer came from Portland. So here I am. I missed my family at first but now I have friends who are almost as close as family."

"Your parents still live there?"

"They do, in the same little house they've lived in for forty years. They're retired now. Which means my mom can enjoy her grandkids who live close by."

"You smile when you talk about them. Good family to grow up in?"

"It was."

By this time, they were standing in the lobby of the Paramount Hotel. Nick caressed her cheek with the backs of his curled fingers.

With his touch she lost all interest in her family; couldn't have remembered her sisters' names if he'd asked.

"What do you think? Am I going to ask you up to my room?" He dropped a quick kiss on her forehead.

"I don't know. Are you?" Every cell in her body was concentrated on the feel of his fingers on her face and a desire to taste his mouth.

"If I ask, do you know what you'll say?"

She reached up and took his chin in her hands. After she kissed him, she said, "Did I give the right answer?"

"The elevator's this way."

• • •

She'd been thinking about this ever since yesterday, when they'd had drinks. Would he ask? Of course he would. Should she go? Maybe just have dinner. Which would be stupid, after Washington. But what about Amanda? She'd lied to her friend. Okay, not lied, just not told her the whole story.

Then she'd seen the look in his eyes when she walked into the restaurant, felt his thumb caress the back of her neck as they sat in the bar while she tried to carry on an intelligent conversation. His touch so unnerved her at first she was sure she'd been speechless. And now, with just the brush of his fingers across her cheek, he had her where he wanted her. Where she wanted to be, in the elevator going up to his room.

Which was lovely. A sofa and leather-covered chairs were grouped around a small, glass table. A private patio, furnished with a wrought iron table and two chairs, overlooked the street. On the desk was his MacBook and, beside the desk, leather bags that probably held his camera equipment.

And, of course, there was a huge king-size bed.

Her expression must have changed because he said softly, "Second thoughts, Fee?"

"Not second thoughts about being here with you, no. But about…" She sighed and made an impatient gesture. "I'm just not very good at this kind of lying."

"Lying? To who?"

"Amanda. I told her we had dinner a few times and I saw your show in Alexandria. That's not true."

"Yes, it is."

"But I didn't tell her everything."

"If she weren't my sister what more would you have told her?"

"A lot more."

"So, women do talk to one another about what goes on in bedrooms."

"Well, not all the details, but sometimes. Don't men?"

"I guess. Mostly when we're immature, stupid teenagers and then it's mostly exaggerated. I'm neither, so I don't." He dropped his hands. "But if you've changed your mind…"

She took a step closer and took his face in her hands, loving the rough feel of his stubble against her skin. "Being here with you like this is all I've thought of since you called. I'm just torn about Amanda."

This time when he put his hands on her waist he pulled her close. "My sister knows exactly what's going on, Fee. I've never come to Portland on a shoot before. The few times I've been here, I've always stayed at her house. I've never had 'a previous engagement' when she asked me to have dinner with her. She knows. And she must be okay with it or I'd have heard about it."

Fiona laughed. "So you think we have her seal of approval?"

"Does it matter so much to you?"

"Her friendship matters to me, yes."

"She's lucky to have such a loyal friend." He kissed her forehead. "Can I convince you to transfer some of your loyalty to other members of her family?"

In place of an answer, she stood on tiptoes and claimed his mouth in a kiss.

• • •

He could feel her heart beating fast and hard, racing from the kiss as much as his own was. When he'd caught his breath, he began to slip the sweater she wore off her shoulders. "This is my second favorite part of having you in my bedroom," he murmured as he unzipped her dress.

She shrugged her shoulders and the dress slithered down her arms and over her hips to the floor. "What's your favorite part?" The glint in her now dark blue-gray eyes said she knew.

"We're getting there, beautiful. We're getting there."

The lacy panties and bra she was wearing held his attention for a few seconds but no longer. He unhooked her bra with a flick of his wrist, making her laugh.

"Hey, this is serious stuff," he said as he lowered the straps of the bra over her shoulders, and he could admire the creamy skin and soft pink nipples he'd uncovered.

"Do I want to know how you got to be so good at unhooking bras?"

"When I was about fourteen, I stole one of Amanda's and practiced." He was kissing his way from her cheek to her now naked breasts.

She detoured him with one hand so she was looking into his eyes. "Not possible."

"How do you know?" He removed her hand and pressed his mouth to her neck. "You weren't there. And Amanda never knew."

"Amanda was in college here in Portland when you were fourteen," she said in her best reporter's "gotcha" voice.

It made him chuckle and almost—*almost*—made him forget what he'd been headed for; her beautiful breasts. "Hush. That's my story and I'm sticking to it."

Kissing between her breasts, then trailing his fingers over her nipples, he was rewarded with her shiver of anticipation. Softly, just barely touching her, he went south, dispensing with her panties just as efficiently as he had the bra.

When he had all her clothes on the floor, he led her to the bed and pulled down the spread. She curled up in the sheets as he made short work of his own clothes, eager to get into bed, into her.

"One of these times, it'll be my turn to undress you first," she said as he slid in beside her.

"Any time you want to undress me, I'd be happy to cooperate, believe me."

She was smiling when he began to nibble his way from her neck to her earlobes and then to her mouth where he converted her smile to a hot, open-mouthed kiss. His hand found her breast, massaging the nipple to a taut point, then skimmed down to grip her hip and pull her against his erection.

"You're all I've thought of since I knew I was coming to Portland." He moved to the other breast, first with his hand, then with his mouth, sucking, licking, nipping at the sensitive skin until he felt her arch her back, pressing against him.

Then he moved down, a kiss at a time, from her breasts to her belly, circling her navel with his tongue, caressing her body with his hands, retracing his steps of a few minutes before until his mouth and hands found the place he wanted, hidden in the folds of her sex.

Gently, one finger found the hot, wet core of her, then another. Then with his fingers inside her and his tongue on her clitoris, he first felt—then heard—her climax.

Kissing his way back up her body, feeling the friction of her soft skin against his hair-roughened chest, he reached her face and in quick succession, kissed her forehead, her eyes and her mouth.

She opened her eyes, began to speak but stopped and just kissed him. She skimmed her hand down his side, then between their bodies. When he realized what she was doing he moved to give her access so she could stroke his cock, slowly at first, then beginning to build in speed and pressure as he felt himself get harder and harder. "God, Fee, you have no idea how good you feel there."

"Not my sweet young thing tonight, are you?" she whispered, then giggled.

"I'll show you sweet young thing, lady," he said and flipped them both so she was on top of him, straddling his hips. He rummaged under the pillow until he found the condom he'd stashed there in anticipation of just this moment and handed it to her. "Here, we're going to need this in about two minutes."

She ripped open the packet and made a move as if to put it on him. But before she had even begun to cover him, she stopped, put the condom aside and slid down his body until she was between his legs. Holding his gaze with hers, she took his penis in her hand and licked her lips. The look she gave him was almost enough to finish him, so lascivious, so erotic, so fucking sexy was it. He didn't think it could be hotter but when she stopped licking her lips and licked him, the temperature went high enough to burn him. He closed his eyes, all his attention focused on her very busy mouth around his rock hard penis as she licked and sucked him until he didn't think he could stand it any longer.

Seeming to know when she'd pushed him to the limit of his control, she looked up at him as she felt around for the condom, the wicked smile back again. As soon as she unrolled the rubber over him, he lifted her by the hips so she was over him and slowly lowered her body onto his. Her moan as he entered her was all he needed to thrust deep into her again and again, as she rode him to her second orgasm. With only a few more thrusts, he poured himself into her.

• • •

Hours later, after another round of sex, they lay side by side. She wanted more than anything to stay wrapped in his arms for the night but she knew she couldn't. "You're a very special man, Mr. St. Claire."

"I'm glad you think so, Ms. McCarthy. Because I think you're one hell of a woman."

She dropped a quick kiss on his mouth and sat up. "But, special as you are, I have to get home."

"Wow, I've heard of fuck and run, but I've never been the victim."

It was all she could do to keep a straight face. "That's not what I'm doing, Nick, and you know it. It's late, I have an early morning breakfast with a source and I can't go to the meeting dressed in the same clothes I had on when I left the office tonight…last night."

"Your source would know?"

"My editor, who's included in the meeting, would. He saw what I changed into before I left to meet you. And I'd never hear the end of it if I showed up in this dress."

"Must be important for both of you to be there."

"It is." She hesitated, not sure how much she wanted to share, but then added, "I'll tell you all about it tomorrow night if you're still interested."

"Can't. I'm headed to the Washington coast tomorrow. I'll be back sometime early Friday. Are you around on Friday night for dinner or something?"

"I have theater tickets for Friday."

"Oh." He frowned.

She was perversely happy to hear the disappointment in his voice. "Want to go with me? My usual theater partner's out of town."

Relief replaced the frown. "Absolutely. What's the play?"

"One of my favorites: *The Importance of Being Earnest*."

"Thank God. Not a musical. Dinner before?"

"How about downstairs? I'll meet you here about six."

"Good." He sat up, too. "Now, let's get dressed and I'll walk you to your car."

"Big girl here who can find her car by herself."

"I'm sure you can, but I don't like to have a woman I care about out on the street alone at this hour. Even in Portland."

They dressed almost as quickly as they had undressed and went out into the spring night with their arms around each other. She really didn't pay much attention to what was around her, her mind filled with pleasure at having Nick so close to her.

"Shall I call when I get back?" he asked.

"Please, so I'll know you didn't get washed out to sea." She looked up at him. "I sound perilously close to your sister, don't I?"

He kissed her lightly on the temple. "Yup, but I hope you have a different reason for wanting me in one piece."

They had reached the corner of the block where she'd parked. Fiona stepped into the street to cross. From out of nowhere a car came speeding down the dark, narrow street. With cars parked on both sides Fiona didn't have many places to get out of the way.

Nick grabbed her and pulled her back onto the sidewalk. Holding her close for a long moment afterward, he finally said, "See? I told you I needed to walk you to your car. You could have been hit."

"It was just some drunk. Where are the cops when you need them?"

"I'll ask Sam the next time I see him," Nick said as they continued the walk to her car.

Chapter 9

"Fiona, let's go. We can't be late. You have everything you need?" Ben Stern was standing over her, the emotion in his normally soft and reasoned voice reflecting his excitement.

"Yup, I'm ready." She slung her bag over her shoulder and headed toward the door. "How the hell did you convince the attorney to let him talk to us? You'd think a high-priced mouthpiece would keep a client accused of shooting at the mayor from talking to anyone before the trial."

"I'm not sure his attorney knows. Preston Garland himself called. Wanted to meet at the Starbucks at Pioneer Courthouse Square. Says if he doesn't see us there at the exact time he mentioned, he'll go to another paper."

They arrived at the coffee shop to find only one empty table and no one to interview.

"Damn." Stern looked at his watch. "We are here at the right time. What the fuck?"

His phone rang. He answered, listened for a few seconds, said, "We got here on time…" but was interrupted. She watched him go to the door and look outside, wave at something—someone—then return to the table. "Okay, we'll be there." He ended the call and motioned to Fiona to follow him.

"What's up?"

"He's playing spy games. He says to come across the street to Nordstrom's and he'll take us to a 'secure location' where we can talk."

"What kind of nut job is he?" she asked as they waited for the light to turn green.

"The kind who will make a great story for the next edition of the paper."

They crossed Broadway and joined Preston Garland, who wore the same jeans and T-shirt he'd been photographed in after he shot up the City Council chambers. He exhibited a level of over-excitement in his long strides that had Fiona almost running to keep up.

Garland led them a few streets away, zigzagging block by block, crossing streets unnecessarily, to the Park Blocks where he picked out a bench for them. Stern raised an eyebrow at her and she nodded in agreement. A bench in a city park wasn't exactly the 'secure location' she'd been picturing either.

When they'd settled the ground rules—he allowed notes but no recording, would only give them twenty minutes, and wanted to make a statement first before they got to the questions—the interview began. He started with a long, rambling speech about how "we" were losing control of our country to "them" and how the white man had to stand up for his rights and protect white women from "them."

The speech included significant amounts of disgusting racial epithets, stereotypes and insults, and Garland seemed to be on the verge of taking up the whole twenty minutes when he suddenly ran out of steam and stopped talking.

"I'm not clear on who 'we' is. Could you be more specific?" Fiona asked.

"Of course I mean the Aryan peoples who settled this country and made it great."

"Mr. Garland," she said, "why does that explain your reason for shooting the mayor?"

"She doesn't belong there and there was no other way to get rid of her."

"She was elected…"

"By people who don't know any better."

"Are there people in Portland who do know better?"

"Of course there are. A few enlightened men who should be in charge."

"Mind telling me who?"

He smirked and crossed his arms over his chest. "Why don't you show me how smart you are by telling me who you think I mean and I'll let you know if you're correct."

Fiona looked at Ben, who nodded. "How about Duke Wellington? Is he one of the people who know better?"

"He certainly could be. He knows what makes the city tick."

"J. H. Ondsdorph?"

"A fine business man and great patriot."

"Sherman Bischler?"

"Absolutely. He certainly belongs in any group of leaders. He's head and shoulders above most of the city's politicians."

"I thought you said you'd tell me if I was correct?"

"Perhaps you're not as smart as you think you are. If you were, you'd know exactly how to read my answers."

"Do you think Wellington, Ondsdorph, or Bischler are the kind of people who could run the city better?"

"Of course they could. There are people in city government already who could do a better job, who aren't happy with the way things are going."

"Staff people or elected officials?"

"People."

"You're not being very specific here, Mr. Garland."

"You're not asking the right questions, Miss McCarthy."

"What's the right question?"

"I'm not stupid enough to fall for your tricks."

"How about going on record about who's paying your attorney, then. I hear he's very expensive."

"The friends who are supporting me in this endeavor have been generous but prefer to remain anonymous."

"Paying you for what you did in City Hall?"

"Supporting me in this endeavor." He looked at his watch. "I see our time has expired. I hope this helps you understand what I did. I'm only sorry I failed at my attempt to remove her from office. The next person will have better luck." He rose from the park bench and walked away.

"Not exactly what I hoped we'd get," Stern said.

"No, but we have the 'next person' comment to play with and if I talk to a few other folks, maybe in the DA's office and in City Hall, I think we can still get a decent story out of this."

"One of the reasons I love having you around, Fiona, is you can always make a silk purse out of a sow's ear."

"Preston Garland is more than just the ear of a pig. He's the whole porker."

• • •

Dinner and the theater with Nick on Friday ended with him staying at her house so they could get an early start on the next day, when he'd asked her to join him on a trip to Mt. Hood. At 5 A.M. they set out to drive up the Columbia River Gorge, accessing Mt. Hood from the north.

It was a perfect day for his photography. A few early rhododendrons were in bloom. An occasional steam plume vented from inside Mt. Hood. Mt. Jefferson was clearly visible to the south against the cloudless blue sky. Nick got shots of Timberline Lodge and its year-round ski facilities; they did some poking around the little town of Government Camp before heading east to look at campgrounds and lakes.

Fiona drove to the parking area she thought she remembered for Lava Lake, a particularly scenic area where she had camped several times with friends when she first lived in Portland. After they'd hiked in for a while, she had to admit she wasn't sure this was the right place.

"Nothing looks familiar and I sure don't see any signs of a lake. It was a bit remote but not this far off the beaten track."

"It's okay, Fee. I have most of what I want anyway as scouting shots. And the light's wrong for me to get anything I can use for exhibition photos."

"Oh, wait, there's a trail there." She pointed to her left. "Maybe I found it."

"This is the last trail, beautiful. I'm running out of bread crumbs."

She strode ahead, Nick following close behind, but a hundred yards along, the trail curved and as she rounded the corner she stopped suddenly.

"Hey," he said, "put on your brake lights or I'll rear-end you." He patted her bottom. "Although you do have a nice rear end to run into."

She didn't acknowledge his pats or his comments. "What the hell is *that?*" she asked, pointing at a large and expensive-looking building in the trees about fifty yards ahead of them. She was sure the owner probably called it a cabin, but it was just a cabin the way the Empire State Building was just an office building.

It was built entirely of logs with a covered porch wrapped around the front and sides of the structure. Oversized rocking chairs and tables, also built of logs, were spaced along the expanse. It had a green metal roof, now dusted with dead fir needles from a winter's worth of storms, and surprisingly small windows in the front.

"Who the hell owns it, I wonder?" she asked.

"People who build this far into Forest Service land usually don't feel it necessary to have welcome mats out with their names on them," Nick observed.

"I suppose you're right." She walked closer. "Look how big it is. From the lack of weathering in the logs, it can't be more than a year or two old." She turned to Nick, who had stayed behind. "Aren't you curious? I am."

"You're not the kind of reporter who breaks into buildings, are you?"

"No, I'm not, any more than you're a paparazzi. I just want to look in." She called, "Hello, anyone home?" as she neared the cabin. There was no answer. "Hello, the house. Is there anyone there?" Still no response.

By then she was at the foot of the steps to the front porch. She took them two at a time, strode across the porch, and knocked on the door.

"What do you plan to say if someone answers?" Nick asked as he joined her.

"Ask where the lake is, of course. But no one's answering, are they?" She moved to the window beside the door and looked in. "Oh, shit."

"What?" he asked as he joined her.

"Look at all the white power stuff." She pointed to dozens of flags and banners ringed around a huge commons room, which appeared to take up much of the main floor of the building. At the rear was a large open-plan kitchen with a restaurant-size stove and refrigerator. Two sets of steps, one on either side of the cabin, led up to a large balcony forming the ceiling for the kitchen and providing a viewing platform for the common room underneath. There were no visible doors to rooms off the balcony and little room for bedrooms behind the kitchen. It looked more like a conference center than a summer home.

"I see a few flags with crosses and funny hats or something, but nothing Nazi-ish. What makes you think it's white power stuff?"

"White power isn't always neo-Nazi. The funny hat, as you call it, is a type of helmet. The helmet is Spanish, the cross Celtic, and the shield French. Diverse, but of course, all European. It's the symbol of a local hate group."

"Interesting sort of information to have at your fingertips. Want to tell me how you know all that?"

"Maybe later. Right now I want to look around."

"Okay, but if you're correct about this stuff, we shouldn't spend a whole lot of time here. I don't want to run into the owner. It's isolated out here and given what's inside, the owner is not a nice person."

"Before we leave, can you take some pictures of the outside of the cabin and through the windows? I particularly want the flags and the weird chewed up poster on the wall." She indicated what appeared to be a large black-and-white photograph of an unidentifiable subject with most of the center of the photo gone.

"I will if you promise to leave here sometime in the next five minutes. I don't like the feel of this place. And just so you know, I can get good outside images but inside through the windows won't be the best shots."

"This is for research, not publication."

"Okay, go get your curiosity satisfied and let's get out of here."

As Nick worked his way around the cabin taking shots of the inside and out, Fiona followed a trail to a shed as sturdily built as the house and locked tight. Beside it was a chewed-up tree, like the poster in the house. She ran her hand over the bark, wondering what could have caused the damage. A sudden snap, like a branch breaking, in the trees close by startled her, but when a large bird flew overhead, she was relieved. It was just the wildlife.

After inspecting the tree from several angles, she came to the conclusion it had been shot up. By whom? And why? She ran around to the front of the building to take another look inside the front room to see if the poster there might have been the target, but as she turned the corner, she tripped and fell.

"Damn it," she yelled.

"What happened, Fee?" Nick came running and got his question answered. Holding out his hand he said, "Here, let me help you up."

She tried to stand but couldn't put any weight on her right ankle. "Oh, shit." She sank back to the ground.

"Hold on a minute and let me get my camera stowed, then I'll help you up and we'll get out of here." He packed up his equipment in his bag and slung it on his back. Then he carefully helped her up, and put her arm around his neck and his arm around her waist.

"Can you put any weight on it at all?"

"A little."

"Then let's start. Go slowly." He held her tightly and she leaned heavily on his shoulder.

After a few steps she said, "Wait. I want to take another look at the weird poster. The more I think about it, the more I think there's something familiar about it."

"You have about a mile, mile and a half of hopping to get to the car. We need to start now. The sun's disappearing behind some dark clouds and I don't want to get caught in a rain shower."

"Please, Nick. Just a quick peek. It'll only take a minute. It's important."

He sighed and changed their direction so she could maneuver onto the cabin porch and look in. "I need to see from another angle." She started to hop toward another window.

He didn't move which meant she couldn't either. "You've had your quick peek. We're outta here, Fee." His tone left no room for arguing.

But she tried anyway. "Damn it, Nick. This could be important. What would two or three more minutes matter? No one's around anyway."

"We're done." He lifted her from the porch to the first step and then onto the second. "I'm not going to waste any more time poking around here."

Twenty minutes of hopping, resting, and hobbling later, she had to admit he knew what he was talking about. And she told him "You were right. This is hard and taking a long time. I'm really sorry I got us into this. I'm usually better at outdoor stuff."

He laughed. "Don't apologize. It's given me an excuse to get my hands all over you."

She winced as she hobbled along, muttering. "Yeah, 'cause you've needed one, haven't you?"

With all the rest stops, it took them almost forty-five minutes to get to the car but they beat the shower that started five minutes after they got there. Nick made Fiona comfortable in the back of her PT Cruiser with her right leg propped up on the seat cushioned by their jackets. He drove down the mountain, stopping only once for a bag of ice for her ankle and something cold to drink for both of them.

An hour and a half later they were back at her house. Wanting to act as if nothing had happened, she tried to get out of the car, but when she put weight on the sprained ankle, she grimaced.

"Hey, you're supposed to wait for me." Nick hurried around the car and grabbed her.

"I thought I could do it myself."

Nick scooped her up in his arms and started toward her front door.

"Wait. My purse..." He lowered her to grab the bag from the floor of the front seat. As she returned her arms to his shoulders she asked, "You do this with all your dates?"

"Not usually. But then, I don't usually take women out in the woods and get them hurt."

"It's not your fault. I wasn't watching where I walked,—well, ran, actually. I've hiked in the woods enough to know better."

"Why don't you let me feel a little responsible? It might get you a take-out dinner and some help with icing your foot." He set her down gently at her front door and waited for her to fish her keys out of her purse.

"It's a deal. Thanks," she said as she opened the door. "I've got take-out menus from every good restaurant for miles around. More menus than food in the house, actually." Her cat made a run for the outside as soon as she opened the door. "Do you mind corralling Pulitzer? I can't chase her like this."

"Happy to. As soon as I get you settled. Did I tell you last night I like your sense of humor? With her for a pet, whatever happens in your professional career..."

"I can say I have a Pulitzer, yeah."

Leaning on him, she hobbled to the couch in her living room and fell onto it with a sigh. "The take-out menus are over there," she said, pointing to a small table under the window in the dining room.

After he'd herded the cat back into the house and they'd eaten Chinese food he'd ordered, Nick disappeared, saying he would police up the kitchen. When he came back to the living room he asked, "Can I do anything else for you? Do you need anything?"

"I think I'll get some ice and hobble to bed."

"Let me get the ice and help you hobble."

The last thing she needed was to have her stupid mistake compounded by having to rely on him any more for help. She'd do it herself. She stood and tried to take a step toward her bedroom. Her ankle crumpled and she almost fell to the floor, saved only by Nick's quick reflexes.

"Damn it, Fee, let me help." He put her arm around him and slowly walked her to her bedroom where he pulled the comforter down and fluffed up the pillows before gently lowering her to the bed.

"They always recommend a big bag of peas for this sort of icing down. You don't happen to have one in your freezer, do you?" he asked.

"No, who other than a family of four ever has one of those huge bags of frozen veggies? Do you?"

"I doubt any vegetable has ever seen the inside of a freezer any place I've ever lived. Ice cream, ice cubes, ice packs, and the odd bottle of vodka, but never peas."

"Exactly. Luckily there's an ice maker in my refrigerator and plastic bags with zipper-things on them in the drawer near the sink."

"I'll be back in a minute. Are you comfortable?"

"I'm getting there."

When he returned, a bag of ice in one hand and a towel from the bathroom in the other, Fiona was in the middle of her queen-size bed with the sheet pulled up over her breasts and tucked under her arms. She had left her sprained ankle uncovered.

Nick picked up the clothes she'd shed and put them on a nearby chair. "Apparently you got there—comfortable, I mean."

"I figured I'm here for the night so I might as well."

Laying the towel on the bed, he picked up her foot, gently placed it on the towel, and arranged the ice pack. When he was finished, he sat on the edge of the bed close to her. She took his hands and pulled at him so she could sit up. As she did, she let go of the sheet, uncovering her bare breasts. Scooting awkwardly, she got close to him and put her arms around his neck. Something about the way he'd taken care of her since she'd fallen had touched her. He didn't seem like the world-traveling photographer who was in town for a while and needed diversion. He really seemed to care that she'd been hurt and wanted to help. It was a side of him as appealing as his dimples and infectious grin.

"It's lonely here. Won't you join me?"

"Are you sure? Maybe I should leave and let you get a good night's sleep." He moved as if to avoid her hands, but she wouldn't let him.

"I'm sure. But if you don't want the challenge of working around an ice pack and my ankle…"

"I'd never turn down a chance to stay with you. You're why I came to Portland. I just don't want to hurt you."

"You won't."

"You're right. I'd never hurt you." Drawing her close, he kissed her, a long, open-mouth kiss she hoped would go on forever. "I've wanted to do this," he nipped at her lip with his teeth, "all day. You chew your lip when you hike and I wanted to stop walking and nibble on your mouth, too." He traced the outline of her lips with his finger. "When I was supposed to be scouting locations, I was thinking about your mouth. Even took some shots of you doing what I wanted to be doing. Not what I was supposed to be shooting but…"

"Can we discuss your photography later?" She began to pull at the bottom of his T-shirt. "Right now, I'm feeling a little underdressed. Should I ask you to bring me my clothes or…"

He smiled and shook his head. "No, I'll join you." She helped him pull his shirt up and off, running her hands over his chest as she did. After he pitched it in the corner he drew her back to him. This time when he kissed her, his tongue played with hers slowly, lazily building her need for him until she was dizzy with desire. She wanted to have him naked and under the sheet with her. Now. But when she fumbled with the buttons on his jeans she couldn't get them undone.

"I have just learned to hate 501s," she said as he stood up to take off the offending pants.

"I'll keep it in mind the next time I buy jeans."

When he lay down next to her, he pulled her close, saying with a surprise in his voice, "You're overdressed now. How come you still have this on?" He brushed his fingers over the lace at the top of her panties.

"In case you turned me down, I could pretend it's what I slept in," she whispered. She could feel his smile against her skin as he kissed his way to her breasts while rubbing the heel of his hand against the silky fabric between her thighs. She moaned and moved restlessly under his tender assault. He began to back his hand away but she grabbed it, returned it, added one of her hands and, together, they slid her panties over her hips so she could shimmy out of them. But they caught on her bottom.

"Lift your hips," he murmured and slipped off her panties when she did. "Tell me what you want. Show me what you want," he said in a hoarse whisper.

"You. I want you inside me." She kissed him, playing sexy with his tongue, trying to convince him.

"We'll get there. Don't worry. What else do you want?"

"Touch me. Here." She moved his hand to her sex.

There were no more words needed. She was lost in the sensation of his fingers on her, urging her toward the inevitable. Her arms were around him; she could feel the pull and play of his muscles as he stroked her. His warm breath was on her neck, tickling the edge of her ear. He took her close, so close, to climax but not over, as though he wanted her there, waiting for him, so they could go over together.

He shifted her leg out and up and moved between her thighs, already covered with a condom she hadn't seen him open. Then with the pads of his fingers he stroked her mouth until she opened her lips and licked at him, taking the tip of his forefinger into her mouth, sucking it hard, drawing a groan from him.

Replacing his fingers with his mouth, he made love to her with his tongue as he entered her. At first he moved deliberately, pulling almost all the way out before thrusting back into her in a sweet and deliberate torture. Eventually, as the sensations intensified, he abandoned the slow slide in and out and moved faster, pressing himself against her most sensitive spot. In the silence of her room all she could hear were the cries of two people caught in passionate love-making; all she could feel was the slip and slide of their sweat-drenched bodies against each other; all she knew was the steep climb to reach the top until they crashed together.

As she lay nestled against him afterward, she traced on his chest with her forefinger.

He kissed her finger. "Want me to get it tattooed?"

"What?"

"Your name. Aren't you writing your name? Should I get a tattoo of it? Then we'll both be pierced and inked."

"You're too sensible to do anything like that."

"Not when it comes to you." He drew her closer and stroked her back.

What the hell did he mean by that?

Chapter 10

She felt Nick kiss the back of her neck. There were worse ways, she decided, to start the day than to have someone so decidedly male spooned around your back. "Have you been awake long? You should have wakened me." She turned to kiss him back.

"I was enjoying the scenery. You're even beautiful when you're asleep." He touched her cheek with the back of his hand. "How's your ankle feel this morning?"

"My ankle?" All she could feel was the touch of his hand on her face and the rest of his body pressed against her.

"The one you twisted yesterday. Or was the ankle just an excuse to hang on to me and get me to carry you into your house?"

"Oh, my ankle. Right." She rotated it under the sheet. "It hardly hurts at all and it doesn't feel swollen. The ice seems to have worked wonders."

"I'm not sure it was the ice. We shouldn't discontinue the other treatment until we know for sure what helped. It's one of the things my mother the doctor taught me." He brought her closer, his erection against her as he nuzzled her neck.

"Sex is therapeutic?"

"Not with anyone, just with me."

She believed him.

Eventually she suggested breakfast and called dibs on the first shower. By the time he'd had his turn; she had dried her hair, wrapped her ankle in an elastic bandage, and was wearing a green cotton robe.

He glanced at her then at the towel he had wrapped around his hips. "If robes are the dress for breakfast, do you have one I could borrow? Preferably not the one with ruffles in the bathroom."

"I have an old terry cloth one in the back of my closet. It will be a little short but should probably work."

He went into her walk-in closet and came out with a brown and cream striped cotton robe. "How about this one?"

That one? The one I never wanted to see again? How the hell did he find that one? She grabbed it from him. "Not that one. I didn't mean…it's not…you can't…" She threw the robe into the back of the closet, found the terry cloth one for him, then turned away.

He put the robe on, tied the belt around his waist and came up behind her. "I'm sorry. What upset you?" He put his hands on her shoulders and attempted to turn her around but she shook him off. "Fiona, what's this about? Tell me. Please."

"Nothing. It's nothing. Just a big mistake." She wiped her eyes on her sleeve and started for the hall.

"Wait." He grabbed her by the arm. "You can't just cry and leave the room."

"I'm not crying."

"Of course you are. Tell me what I did so I won't do it again." This time when he tried to turn her around, she let him.

"It's just, like I said, a mistake. You didn't do anything."

"It's hard to believe from your reaction." He tilted her chin up but she refused to meet his eyes. "A mistake?" He paused for a moment. "Was the mistake what makes you keep the shades down on those eyes and made you decide you needed body art?"

Shaking her chin free of his hold, she put her forehead on his chest and felt him wrap his arms around her. "I'm not good at serious discussions before I have coffee. Can we have breakfast?"

After a few breaths he said, "Okay, let's have breakfast," and followed her to the kitchen.

Not sure she could actually make omelets with him watching her so intently, she suggested he put some music on and pointed him in the direction of the living room shelves where she knew he'd find distraction. And, indeed, after he rummaged through what he found, he called into the kitchen, "I can't believe you have all these old records. Where'd you get them?"

She came out wiping her hands on a dishtowel. "Most of them belonged to my parents. They got rid of their turntable, got an iPod and downloaded their music from the '60s and '70s from iTunes. I love old vinyl, scratchy sounds and all, so I took the records before my mother could throw them out. And I add to them when I find something I really like."

"Some of them look like they could be worth something."

"No, my father had a dealer go through them. They'd been played so much, the records and especially the album covers weren't in good enough shape for collectors who, apparently, want mint-condition albums."

"What's your favorite?"

"Probably Crosby, Stills, and Nash."

He held up the *Déjà Vu* album. "I must have sensed the vibe."

"Wrong vibe. You've got Crosby, Stills, Nash, *and Young*."

He flipped through a few more albums and came across the right one. In a few minutes, the sounds of "Suite: Judy Blue Eyes" came from the four speakers around her living room.

While they ate the omelets she'd made, they talked music: Fiona's favorites from her parents' youth—Simon and Garfunkel, Creedence Clearwater Revival, Chicago, Bob Dylan, the Eagles. How her mother and father had been arguing for years over who was better, the Beatles or the Stones. She confessed she went to all the old guys' reunion concerts and loved them even if they couldn't hit the notes as well as they did when they made the records she owned. Nick shared about the music he'd come to love visiting the Caribbean and Asia and urged her to listen to Yo Yo Ma's *Silk Road* albums.

They finished their coffee and Fiona collected the plates so she could wash them. She was about to get up from the table when Nick reached out to stop her, broaching the subject she had hoped had been forgotten. "Fiona, before you do the dishes, can we talk about what happened in your bedroom?"

"I guess I owe you an explanation, but I'm just not sure…" She shook off his hand and took the dirty plates to the sink. He followed her. She stood for a moment with her back to him and then turned with a sigh. "I'm sorry I freaked about a bathrobe. Not exactly the reaction you expect the morning after an amazing night, is it?"

"It was a little surprising."

"It's just…well, you were right. He…the guy who owns… wore…the robe is the one who…well, he…" She took a deep breath. "I don't know how much detail I want to get into."

"I'm not looking for details; I just want to understand what's going on."

She collected her thoughts then said, "The nut 'graph is, the guy who owned the robe, who said he was in love with me, who I fell for pretty hard…" She paused, picked up her coffee mug, and took a gulp. "This guy, after we'd been together for a few years, moved to Seattle to marry the woman he'd been engaged to most of the time we were together and who was the mother of a daughter I didn't even know he had."

"Fucking asshole. I'm sorry something I did brought it all back." Nick put his arms around her, saying softly, "Why'd you keep it?"

She didn't answer because she didn't know what the answer was.

"Never mind. But I can take it with me, if you'd like, and get rid of it for you."

She shook her head, not meeting his gaze. "No, thanks. I have to…I'll take care of it myself."

He let go of her and kissed her forehead. "Just so you know, you're not alone in the bad relationship department. I don't have any tattoos to show for mine and, in my case, it's my fault, I guess."

"You don't have to do this, Nick."

"You were honest with me; I'll be honest with you. About a year ago, the woman I'd been with for awhile, a videographer I've worked with a lot, broke it off because I was, and these were her exact words, more interested in getting a good angle for my shot than I was in making our relationship work. The last straw, she said, was when I cancelled the fourth plan we had for going away together because a good assignment came up. I had no idea she was keeping score. And I thought she understood about my job. But she was, she didn't, and she was pissed."

Fiona nodded. "The old 'you don't love me as much as you do your job.' I've been there too, with a guy I dated when I first worked for *Willamette Week* and was trying to impress the editor. I thought Robe Guy was different. He was another reporter and understood my job."

He pulled her closer again and kissed her gently. "Thing is, she wasn't the first to call the issue to my attention. I haven't been exactly the best guy to be with."

"It's okay, Nick…"

"No, it's not. Because I don't want to be like that with you." His hands on her shoulders, he caught her gaze with his and said, "This—whatever's going on between us—is…well, I don't know what it is. But it feels different. I want to find out what it is. Do you?"

She buried her head in his shoulder so he couldn't see the fear in her eyes. "I don't know. I'm scared of those kinds of questions."

"We're great together."

"Yes, we are."

"So, do you want to find out what it is?"

She answered by pulling his mouth to hers, her hand on the back of his neck. The kiss started out sweet and gentle but rapidly moved to something more intense—something deep and passionate. She was about to say she didn't know how to answer him with words when the phone rang.

He held her to keep her from picking up the receiver and shook his head, but when her phone announced the call was from Margo Keyes, she insisted. "I have to take it. Margo and I had tentative lunch plans today and she's probably calling about it."

"Can you reschedule? I'd like to spend the rest of the day with you."

"Let me see what she has to say."

As soon as Fiona answered the call, Margo launched into an explanation of how she was stuck at work making preparations for a trial on Monday and asking forgiveness for begging off from lunch.

"It's okay, Margo, don't worry. We can have lunch some other time."

"Thank you. We can reschedule after this trial's over. I'll call you later this week and let you know how it's going."

Nick had come up behind her and was kissing the back of her neck, his hand under the front of her robe caressing her breasts. She pulled away from him, mouthing, "stop it" before responding to Margo. "Next week. Right. Good. How's Tony, by the way? I didn't get much chance to talk to him at Higgins the other night."

"He's fine. Well, except someone told him a real Oregonian recycles everything. So, now he inspects every wastebasket before I dump it to make sure I'm not throwing out something recyclable. It has the potential to become wearing. Otherwise, life's good."

Fiona laughed but before she could say anything, Margo continued. "Oh, I almost forgot, Amanda called last night asking if I knew where you were. I think she was actually looking for Nick. She said he was shooting alone on Mt. Hood and she was concerned she couldn't reach him. After the conversation at Higgins you'd think she would be embarrassed enough to leave it alone, but I guess she's not."

"Amanda needn't have worried. Nick didn't go to Mt. Hood alone. I went with him. And I imagine he'll call her soon." She motioned to Nick who headed for the bedroom.

"Because…"

"Because what?"

"You imagine he'll call her soon because he's there with you and heard what you said?"

"Something like that."

"And Amanda couldn't reach him last night because he'd turned his phone off so the two of you wouldn't be interrupted?"

"Something like that."

"So that's why you were so gracious about my cancelling our lunch. Now you can spend today with him, too. But since I don't want to hear 'something like that' again, I'll refrain from saying it in the form of a question. Now I *know* we need to reschedule. Soon."

A few minutes after she wound up her call with Margo, Nick came back from his phone call to his sister.

"Did you pacify Amanda?" she asked.

"I think so. She knew—or said she knew—you were with me so she didn't really need much calming down. She asked us for dinner tomorrow with Margo and Tony. I said yes because she didn't give me a lot of room to say no. I hope you don't mind. Our assignment is to bring an appetizer."

"No, it's fine." She chewed her lip as she continued. "So, we're definitely outed."

"They saw us at dinner at Higgins. She knows I'm with you now. You said you wanted to be honest with her, didn't you?"

"Yeah, I know. But now it's real and I'm not so sure."

He moved close to her and pulled on the sash of her robe until it came untied and slipped his hands around her bare waist. "You, lady, are hard to please. But maybe I can convince you it's okay." He kissed her and put his hands on her bottom, pressing her hips against his. She looped her arms around his neck and he kissed her again; this time he did the nibbling on her lips. She made little noises at the back of her throat when he played with her tongue, molding her body to him.

When he started kissing his way down her cheek and neck, she said, "If we keep this up, I won't have any skin left anywhere tomorrow. I already have whisker burns on my face, my neck, my breasts, and other places I'm afraid to look."

"Next time I'm there, I'll let you know." He kept on kissing her, now reaching the top of her breast.

"You're terrible."

"Am I?" His head came up, on his face a look of mock surprise.

"No, actually, you're wonderful."

"I'm relieved. But I promise I'll be more careful." To demonstrate he could be, the kiss was gentle but no less intense as his mouth lingered on hers and he held her close. "Maybe like so?"

"Oh, God, Nick, when you kiss me I don't care if you sand off the whole upper layer of my skin."

"I had something in mind a little less like cosmetic surgery or wood shop." He released her from his arms. "We could see what we can work out until it's time for me to change clothes and get my other camera. I want to get some shots from Mt. Tabor at sunset tonight. Want to go with me?"

"Today I think I'd follow you to the moon."

"I have a closer destination in mind," he said as he pulled her toward her bedroom.

Chapter 11

"Mommy, I think it's Uncle Nick. Can I open the door?"

"Wait 'til I get there, kitten."

Fiona and Nick could hear the conversation between his four-year-old niece Kat and her mother after they rang the doorbell. Kat wasn't supposed to open the door unless there was an adult with her, but it didn't stop her from asking every time if she could.

When the door was flung open, Kat threw herself at Nick.

"Uncle Nick! Did you bring me a present?"

Amanda started to reprimand her daughter but Nick headed it off by picking up his niece and hugging her before handing her a small bag.

"Of course I did, Kat. I brought you a Balinese dancer from Indonesia."

While Kat tore the bag to get at the present inside, Chihuly, the family's curly coated retriever, joined the welcoming party, sniffing at both Nick and Fiona, wagging his tail when Fiona petted him.

Amanda kissed Fiona's cheek and said, "Please forgive my daughter. Nicky has her spoiled. He brings her a doll from each place he visits." She turned to her brother. "Hey, baby brother, how are you?"

Nick kissed his sister. "Just as fine as when you asked yesterday."

To her daughter Amanda said, "Kat, please say hello to Fiona, too."

"Hello," Kat said. She looked at her uncle and then at Fiona. "Are you Uncle Nick's girlfriend?"

"Sarah Katherine Richardson!" her mother said.

"It's okay, Amanda," Fiona said ignoring Nick's snort as he attempted to hide his grin behind his niece's curls. "Let me think about it for a minute, Kat. Okay, let's see, I'm a girl." She held up one finger. "Your Uncle Nick is my friend." She held up a second finger. "So, I guess I'm his girl friend," pausing between the last two words and holding her hand up, palm outward, for a high-five.

"Well, if you're his girlfriend, why don't you marry him? Then you'd be my Aunt Fiona."

"This is why we try to stop her at the first appalling statement. If you don't, it just gets worse," Amanda said. "Kat, we don't ask people about personal things, remember?"

"Okay, Mommy." Kat had begun patting Nick's face. Now she scrutinized him carefully. "Why do you look different, Uncle Nick?"

"I don't know. Maybe you forgot what I looked like because it's been a while since I've seen you."

Amanda looked at him curiously. "Kat's right, Nicky, you do look different. What have you…? Oh, my God, you finally learned how to shave properly."

"All right, Amanda. Now it's your turn to keep it down," he said.

Amanda led the couple into the living room to join her husband, Tony, and Margo. "Look, Sam, Nicky finally learned how to shave."

"This is what I love about my family. Five minutes into the evening and my niece and my sister have already embarrassed both me and my date," Nick muttered.

"I'd forgotten you were halfway decent-looking underneath all the fuzz," Sam said as he stood so he could clap his brother-in-law on the back. "Still not in my class but not bad for a kid."

"I'm curious, Nicky, why, after Mom and I have begged you for months to shave, have you finally done it?" Amanda asked.

Tony grinned. "It's what Fiona and Margo have in common, isn't it? I have to do the same thing. Although not as much as I used to." He turned to Margo. "Are we turning into a boring old married couple, sugar?"

"Can I get these appetizers organized?" Fiona asked, desperate to change the subject. "Amanda, do you have a plate I can use to put out the bruschetta?"

"Oh, you brought my favorite," Margo said, her desire to move onto something else to talk about almost as strong as her friend's. "Let me help."

The two women headed for the kitchen with Amanda following.

"What's Tony talking about?" Amanda asked as she got down a large platter and handed it to Fiona.

"It's our Irish skin. It's easily…well…it's easy to…" Fiona began as she tried to hide her red face by busying herself pulling out toasted bread slices, mozzarella cheese, and a container of chopped and seasoned tomatoes.

"Oh, hell, Amanda, Nick probably shaved so Fiona isn't covered in whisker burns all the time," Margo said as she plucked basil leaves from their stems and put them on the bread slices. "When we were first together I sometimes asked Tony to shave twice a day, particularly on weekends so I didn't show up in court with my face red and peeling like some horny teenager. *His* face got irritated from shaving so much until he started using an electric razor occasionally. It's not so bad now. Either my skin has toughened up or we're turning into the boring old married couple he mentioned."

Amanda burst out laughing. "No wonder my mother and I couldn't make Nicky shave. Thank you, Fiona. I hated his grubby, stubbly look. Wait 'til I tell Mom. She'll send you flowers."

"The thing is, I kinda liked it," Fiona said. "And I never asked him to. He did it all on his own this morning."

Nick appeared in the door to the kitchen with two glasses of wine in his hands. "Is it safe to come in here?"

"Yes, Nicky. I'll stop talking about your face," Amanda said.

"Thank God. Now all I have to worry about is Kat. Wine, Fee?" He offered her a glass.

"Thank you, yes." She looked up at him as she took the glass from him. His fingers brushed hers, their eyes held, unconsciously she took a deep breath and made a small sound of contentment as he formed his lips into the fleeting wisp of a kiss and touched his wine glass to hers. Margo and Amanda simultaneously turned away as if to give them privacy.

When he'd left the room, Margo put her arm around her friend. "I love seeing you like this." She kissed her cheek. "It's been way too long since you've looked happy."

"I am happy," Fiona said. "I've decided it's time to stop moping and get on with my life."

"Not that I don't love my brother but you should know he has the reputation of leaving on the next plane for some assignment or other," Amanda said. "I wouldn't want you to get hurt again."

"We're just having a good time. I won't get hurt," Fiona said, not sure if she was trying to convince her two best friends—or herself. "He's a great guy and he won't leave Portland with me pissed off at him. I promise you."

"What I want to know is, how come he gets away with calling you Fee? No one else can," Margo said.

"I've never liked being called Fee. But when Nick does it..." She smiled and shrugged her shoulders. "I don't know. It's just different, somehow."

Margo hugged her again, then wiped at her eyes with a napkin. "Okay, let's get these bruschetta out there. This is turning into a weepy chick session." She headed for the living room with the appetizers and the other two women followed with plates of cheese and crackers.

Kat was in her glory for another half hour going from Tony to her Uncle Nick to her daddy, begging for bites of cheese and bruschetta, getting plenty of attention, while Chihuly followed her scarfing up the crumbs she let fall to the floor. When Amanda announced dinner was imminent, Sam took Kat upstairs to bed after five minutes of dramatic goodnight kissing and hugging. The adults went into dinner on his return.

After finishing their meal, Margo and Amanda went to the kitchen to make coffee. Everyone else went into the living room.

"Fiona," Sam said before she could settle on the couch, "while I have a chance to do this when my wife can't see I'm turning a social evening into business, would you mind talking with me for a minute?" He gestured toward the sunroom where the family's home office was located. Fiona looked at Nick with a "do you mind" expression. He shook his head; she followed Sam and, with the last of her wine from dinner, sank into the comfortable chair he pulled over to the desk for her.

"I heard you had an interview with Preston Garland. Anything I should know?"

"I'll tell you what little I found out if you'll tell me what you can. Off the record, of course."

When Sam nodded his head, she continued. "I had twenty minutes with Mr. Garland, who was quite proud of what he did. It was hard to hold my tongue when he was ranting on about how 'those people' are taking over and white men—he was specific about it being men—had to do something about it."

"Yeah, I was in on some of the questioning before he got out on bail. He made me want to throw up—or punch him in the nose."

"How the hell did he get out on bail, anyway? Isn't someone who shot at the mayor someone who should be in jail until his trial?"

"You and I may think so but Judge Grayson didn't. Garland has ties to the community and no record of any kind so the good judge didn't believe he was a flight risk. The DA argued against it but lost. When he asked for, and got, an exorbitant bail, the guy's lawyer never even blinked. Garland made bail within an hour."

"When I talked to him, he seemed to be trying to get me to guess who was providing the money for him and the organization behind him," she said. "I threw a couple names out—Duke Wellington, Sherman Bischler, and J. H. Ondsdorph—and he kinda smirked at me. Never could get him to confirm anything, but he seemed to want me to believe one or the other of them was involved somehow."

"He give you any indication of an insider in City Hall who was involved?"

"He said not everyone in City Hall was happy with the way the mayor was running things. No names, just said someone on the inside was disgruntled. You're still working from the theory someone on staff brought the gun into the building, right?"

"Yeah, Garland will only say a friend gave it to him. He says he brought it in with him, but the images from the security camera show him going through the metal detector clean." He crossed his leg over his knee and nodded so she'd go on.

"One last thing from the interview. He said he was only sorry he failed, but he was sure the next person wouldn't."

"I'll pass it along to the mayor's security detail, although I'm not sure they can get much more vigilant. The mayor's already complaining about how intrusive they are. Nothing else?"

"From the interview, no. And FYI, most of it will be in next week's edition." She waited to see if he objected. He didn't so she went on, "I'm still working on the white power angle. The Southern Poverty Law Center says they don't know anything about the White Knights group. They're not on their list of hate groups in Oregon. They list ten in case you didn't know."

"Now eleven. Just what we need, a new group of crazies to stir things up."

"Exactly." She squirmed in her chair. "I'm sure there're connections between the assassination attempt, the White Knights, and one of the three men. They all opposed Mayor Carter's election and backed her opponent with big bucks."

"True of at least half, maybe more, of the business people in the city because she campaigned on raising business taxes."

"I know but the thing is, most of the business community started working with her after she was elected. These three haven't."

"Still, you've got nothing—other than a smirk from our perp—to link any of them to the attempted assassination."

"And it's making me nuts. There is one other thing, although I don't know what it means. When Nick and I were on Mt. Hood we came on a huge cabin tucked away in a remote area. I was curious so I went and looked in the windows. Downstairs in this big room were all sorts of white power flags, including some with the White Knights logo. Nick took some photos of the place. I'm going to try to track down who owns it."

"Still nothing illegal or linked to either the assassination attempt or your three businessmen."

"I know. All I have are these little shreds of things. I feel like there's something important I've already seen or heard, but it keeps slipping away from me." She slid to the edge of her chair. "I think Nick has his digital camera with him. You want to see the shots he took? Maybe something will strike you."

"Sure, I'll take anything at this point to give me some traction."

"So you don't have anything for me?" She couldn't sound disappointed because she hadn't really thought he did.

"Garland hinted he had ties to a group like the White Power Knights. But he did the same thing with us he did with you—lots of innuendo; no facts. We know he has a history of involvement in some odd groups."

"Like what?"

"A defunct neo-Nazi group in Idaho, a white power group in Spokane, some anti-government group in Kansas. He seems to have spread himself out, as an acquaintance of mine used to say, all over hell and half of Georgia."

"Where's he from?"

"Walla Walla originally but he lived all over the place for about ten years. Then, a couple years ago, he moved back in with his parents out in Clackamas County." He fiddled with a pen on the desk. "He doesn't seem to have regular work, which is interesting, given the cost of his high-powered attorney who specializes in representing white power groups. Unfortunately there aren't disclosure laws for who pays the mouthpiece so we don't know who's footing the bill."

"Anything else?" Fiona asked.

"One thing. Add another name to your list of local business people with possible flakey agendas: Lyle Cochran. He's been in the mayor's face about renaming Broadway and a couple other issues, and he may have met with Garland's lawyer when he was in town last week."

"I need fewer people to dig into, Sam, not more. But thanks."

The door to the sun room/office opened and Amanda stuck her head in. "I came to break this up and insist the two of you join us for dessert and coffee. Nicky and I are feeling deserted."

"Sorry, pretty lady. We'll be out in a minute."

Amanda said, "You better be," and withdrew.

Sam stood up. "Keep me posted on what you find. And be careful where you're poking sticks. These people aren't nice."

"Thanks. I will."

"One more thing. It doesn't take a detective to see you're pretty wrapped up in the guy you're with. Fair warning, these St. Claires have a way of getting under your skin. Permanently." He smiled at her. "I should know."

"I'm afraid you're a few weeks too late."

"Thought that might be the case. Don't know what they have but whatever it is it's powerful." His smile turned into a grin as he opened the sunroom door.

Fiona beamed back at him. "Maybe there's some Ohio genetic trait we Northwesterners are particularly susceptible to."

They were both laughing as they joined the other four in the living room. Margo had brought out her contribution to dinner, a plate of fruit and mini tarts, and Amanda was pouring coffee.

Fiona settled herself next to Nick. "What were you and Sam so involved in?" Nick asked as he took her hand and kissed it.

"Sam's working the attempted assassination of the mayor and we were exchanging information. Sorry. I got carried away. It was rude. Forgive me?"

"Nothing to forgive. Was he any help?"

"Not sure either of us helped the other." She ducked her head for a second or so before changing the subject. "Can you give Sam a peek at what we saw on the mountain yesterday? I think he should know about it."

Nick didn't answer at first and she was afraid he was going to ask questions she wasn't sure she wanted to answer just yet but finally he said, "Sure. The digital's in the car. I wanted to show Amanda a couple of the Mt. Hood ones anyway." He leaned in and said quietly enough only she could hear. "Then can we get out of here? I've had enough of sharing you for tonight."

Before Fiona could answer, Amanda said, "If my daughter was here, she'd tell you whiskering isn't polite. Although, come to think of it, I guess we have established Nicky doesn't whisker anymore." She was standing behind them with a coffee pot.

"Sorry, Amanda. No more whispering. I promise," Fiona said, not anxious to resurrect the subject of her skin and Nick's beard.

Amanda offered the coffee. "Like some more?"

Nick put his hand over his cup. "No, thanks, I think we're about to leave."

"Yeah, I bet," Amanda said with a smirk.

"Before you go, can I take a look at those shots Fiona talked about?" Sam asked.

"Sure. Let me go get them," Nick said.

He was only gone a few minutes and came back empty handed. "Not sure what this says about the state of public safety in Portland," he said, looking at his brother-in-law. "Someone broke into my rental car. My camera and all the gear I had with it is gone."

•••

After Sam called in the report of the car prowl, Nick and Fiona returned to St. Johns. They hadn't been home more than fifteen minutes when the phone rang. Nick swore and suggested they ignore it, but the metallic voice on caller ID said it was his sister so she answered it anyway.

It wasn't Amanda. It was Sam.

"We have another complication. Preston Garland was found dead in his parents' garage."

"Jesus. Dead?" She had to swallow hard to clear the knot in her throat before she could say anything else. "How? What happened?"

"It's all conveniently arranged to look like a suicide, complete with a computer generated note saying he didn't want to embarrass his family any further by standing trial."

"Conveniently arranged? You don't think it was a suicide?"

"M.E. says it's not likely. The marks on his neck were likely made by something like a wire ligature, not the rope he was found hanging from. And he says there was no way Garland could have hanged himself from the light fixture—the chair set up to look like the one he used was in the wrong place for him to have kicked it away."

"So you'll be investigating it as a homicide?"

"We're going to let the story ride as a suicide but, off the record, we're investigating it as a homicide, yeah."

"I understand. Thanks for letting me know, though. I might have some use for it one of these days when I get enough to write about."

"I'm not telling you this as a journalist, but as a friend."

"You want me to know these guys play for keeps."

"I have to wonder about the timing of Garland's death. It comes damn close to when he talked to you. And I don't think the break-in of Nick's car was random. So, let me repeat: watch where you're poking sticks."

"You're serious? You think someone was specifically after Nick's camera?"

"Is it possible someone saw you up there on the mountain?"

"I don't think anyone saw us. Why?"

"Someone might want to get rid of any evidence you have."

Fiona shivered. "We still have the evidence. Nick downloaded the images onto his computer before we went to your house."

"Shit. Keep quiet about it. No one should know. Not your boss, not anyone."

"We won't tell anyone."

When she hung up, Nick, who'd been eavesdropping, asked, "So, what aren't we supposed to tell?"

If Sam was right, if Nick's car had been broken into because he'd done a favor for her, it was time to tell Nick about what she was working on. At least, tell him enough so he could stay out of danger.

"Let's go sit down in the living room. There are a couple of things you should know about this story I've been digging into."

They settled on the couch and she started with, "I don't normally talk about my stories before I have a handle on them but this one seems to have gotten more complicated than usual. And it involves you."

"Is this the same story you told me a bit about when we were in D.C.?"

"Yes and no. One of the stories I was working on was about a bill introduced by one of our delegation. But more importantly, one or more of the local supporters of that legislation may be financing a new white supremacist group about to open up shop in Portland."

"A white supremacist group in the People's Republic of Portland? The Northwest bastion of progressives?"

"Most of Portland may be progressive now but it hasn't always been, and Portland isn't Oregon. The militia movement is active in more places than you'd guess and there are almost a dozen hate groups we know about."

"This is why you knew what you were looking at in the cabin."

"Exactly. The rumors about the White Power Knights of the West..."

"That's their name? Could they have picked a dumber one?"

"Yeah, I agree but a dumb name doesn't mean they aren't dangerous. I'm sure there's a connection between their sudden emergence and the election of the city's first black mayor."

"You think they're responsible for the attempt on the mayor's life, don't you?"

"Yup. And for the death of the man arrested for the attempt. That's what Sam's call was about."

"What the hell? Your interview the other day?"

"Yeah, it's supposed to look like a suicide but it's being investigated—quietly and without saying so—as a murder."

"Jesus, Fee, this puts a hell of a target on your back. That car coming out of nowhere the other night and almost hitting you—do you suppose...?"

"I don't know. Maybe. And maybe the car prowl tonight wasn't accidental. Sam thinks we were seen on the mountain and the break-in was to get your images of the cabin."

"Luckily I have them on my computer."

"Which gets us to what no one has to know. If anyone finds out you still have those images, you have a target on your back, too. Are you sure you want to be wandering around the mountains alone?"

Chapter 12

Fiona had gotten nasty emails and tweets, even threatening letters, in response to her articles before but no one she'd ever interviewed had been murdered. And, if Nick was correct about the brush with the car on the Park Blocks, no one had ever tried to hurt her. Or stolen the belongings of someone she was involved with.

What the hell had she set in motion with her digging?

Nick stayed with her for a few nights, thank God, seeming to know she didn't want to be alone. He ferried back and forth to his hotel room to pick up clean clothes and camera gear. Eventually, she more or less told him he could go back to the hotel room he was paying for but not using. She thought she saw disappointment in his eyes but when he immediately began packing his belongings, she decided it was just a trick of light.

They saw each other for dinner every few days. Now that she'd let him in on the details of her story, she shared with him what rocks she was turning over looking for information. He reported his progress with police reports and insurance company forms from the car prowl, showed off the new gear he'd bought to replace the stolen equipment and updated her on the schedule for his work with his buddy Travis whose arrival was getting closer.

Then one evening, as they were prepping dinner together in Fiona's kitchen, he mentioned making plane reservations to leave Portland.

Startled by the depth of her disappointment at the news, Fiona said the first thing she could think of to cover. "So soon? Isn't Amanda upset you're leaving after such a short visit?"

"*Amanda* upset?" He smiled. "I think she's okay with it. She's pretty sure I'll be back soon."

She tried to recover. "Of course, I knew you'd be leaving when the assignment was over. I guess I just didn't think in terms of when."

"I've had the next two on my calendar for months. One's a *National Geographic* photo week in New Mexico; the other's an Alaska cruise. Both of them teaching classes on photography."

Not wanting to continue the conversation about his leaving any further, she went back to something she thought she could handle. "When did you see Amanda?"

"This afternoon when I dropped by her studio."

"Do you always spend time with her in her studio when you come to town?"

"No. I've been there, but this was the first I've spent any amount of time watching what she does."

"I'd love to see how she works some day."

"She'd be happy to have you. Today she was showing off her new series of pieces interpreting landscapes and it gave me an idea. I think we're going to try to put together a body of work based on her interpretations of some of my photos. She thinks Liz Fairchild might be talked into having the exhibit at her gallery."

"What a great idea. And if you got her talking about her work and your project for any amount of time, it must mean she didn't have a chance to give you instructions on how to live your life."

"Hell, no. Stopping her from fussing at me would take an act of Congress…no, an act of God."

"What was it this time? She's already covered being alone on the mountain, so was it taking an umbrella with you when it looks like rain? Wearing your seat belt?"

"It was you."

"Me? She was warning you away from me?" She could tell by his face he was enjoying her surprised reaction.

"On the contrary. She asked me if I knew about your last relationship. Said she didn't want to see you hurt again. Seems like you've also fallen under the protective wing of my sister, who fusses."

Fiona wasn't sure if having Amanda look out for her was a good or bad thing. More accurately, she wasn't sure what Nick thought of it.

Without looking directly at him, Fiona asked, "So, what did you say?"

"I said you'd told me all about it. She was torn between lecturing some more and cross-examining me to find out if I knew any details she didn't. She chose the lecturing option; no surprise." He took his knife to the sink and then washed his hands. "I said she had nothing to worry about. I'd taken it as my job to restore your faith in men." As he dried his hands, he came up beside her.

She laughed. "Big job, isn't it, being responsible for your entire sex?"

"It would be if I meant it. I really only want you to have faith in me." He took her hands. "I want to earn your trust because if I can't, I'll never be able to convince you to…well, to see if we can be more than two people having a vacation fling."

Anxiety began to tense up her shoulders and cramp her hands around the pan she was holding. This conversation was getting into waters too deep for Fiona's comfort. It was bad enough the work she loved seemed to be turning deadly, without having Nick begin to talk about trust and love and things even more dangerous than death threats.

"Nick, I'm not sure I can deal with this yet."

He took the pan from her hands, wrapped his arms around her, and kissed the top of her head. "I get it. You're skittish about a relationship." He held her so she couldn't back away. "But I thought from the way it's been between us, maybe we could see if…"

"We haven't exactly been looking at this…at us…with any sort of reason or common sense, have we?" The panic she had begun to feel when he first talked about earning her trust had now taken over her throat and she had to force out the words.

"Okay, let's talk common sense—we're good together. Right? We share interests. Even our careers mesh. You already know and like some of my family. They like you. Don't you want to see what we can make of a pretty solid beginning? See where it could take us? I do."

"Don't make promises you can't keep, Nick." She had to get away while she could do it with dignity and not when she'd given in to the need to run, to flee this attempt to pin her down, just like Mark had done—before her ex walked away. But Nick wouldn't let go of her.

"Why do you think I won't keep my promise? Is it because you think all men are alike? We're not. I'm not him, Fiona. I know you haven't known me very long, but surely you know me well enough to realize I would never, ever hurt you like he did."

"Stop, Nick. Please. I can't do this." The panic was getting worse. Now tears were threatening.

He looked at her, sighed, and pulled her close. "I'm sorry. I didn't mean to make you cry. I just wanted...just hoped...you might be interested in taking a chance on having something real with me."

"It's not you I'm afraid to take a chance on. It's the uncertainty of things. Of what happens when people..." She stopped before she said anything more compromising and pulled herself away from him. This time, he let her go. She ran to her bedroom and slammed the door.

A few minutes later she heard a soft knock on the door. If she ignored it, maybe he'd go away. She should have known him well enough by now to know it wouldn't work. He kept knocking. "Come in," she finally said.

He sat on the bed next to her where she had curled up like an armadillo trying to protect herself.

"This isn't what I had in mind for this evening," he said. "I'm sorry. Would you rather be alone tonight? I can sleep in the guest room or go back to my hotel."

The thought was tempting, but she couldn't throw him out of her bed, not when her panic was the reason for this, not his behavior. "Why would I force you to fight Pulitzer for the bed in the guest room?"

"Maybe because I wasn't very sensitive out there in the kitchen."

"It's not you, Nick, it's me."

"You're sounding like a *Seinfeld* rerun."

She didn't laugh or even smile. He leaned down and kissed her, then went to the other side of the bed and lay down on top of the comforter. He gently rubbed her back. "Tell me what you need so you feel comfortable with the possibility there's an 'us' worth talking about."

"I just don't know how there can be an 'us.' I still don't even understand why you think you want to spend time with me."

She heard him softly laugh. "Wow. I thought I was more convincing. Or at least interesting enough to warrant your attention."

"You're amazing. I'm the one who barely moves the needle past boring. You travel all over the world, meet interesting people. You can pack in five minutes for anyplace in the world and you probably speak six languages."

"You're describing what I do for a living, not who I am. I think fascinating is knowing more about the city you've lived in for nine years than most people know about a place they've lived all their lives."

"Right. I travel to faraway places like Salem, Oregon, and look at a file some bureaucrat's trying to hide from me. Luckily I don't need a passport to do it because I've never even had one."

"Is lack of a passport the reason you can't see me with you?"

"Of course not. There's our backgrounds. Your parents are professionals. My father worked on the docks. You went to private schools and a trust fund paid for your education. I'm still paying off college loans."

"I'll give you there was more money in my family. But our upbringing wasn't so different. Our families are close, warm, and supportive. In spite of my bitching, I love my sister as much as you love yours. And we both have good relationships with our parents. True?"

"I guess."

"No guess. It's true. What else you got?"

"Why did you want to find me?"

"Find you? When?"

"In D.C. Why? I mean, I understand why you chatted me up at Danny and Jake's engagement party. We were the only two people there who weren't paired up, so you…"

"Talked to you because you were the most beautiful, most interesting woman in the room."

"Oh, please. You didn't call after the party. I couldn't have been that interesting."

"You're the most interesting, most beautiful woman in any room. When you start talking about what you care about, like your job, you absolutely glow. But I couldn't figure out how to contact you without Amanda interfering. Then she told me you were in D.C. and I had my chance."

"You went to a lot of trouble because you admired my passion for my job."

"Obviously there was more. And after the first time I kissed you, there was the other passion I discovered. That one I definitely wanted to know more about."

"So, this is just about sex."

"Fee, are you trying to get rid of me? Is that what this is about?"

"No. God, no. I'm trying to understand how we got here—why you got here—before we try to go someplace else."

"Would it help if I told you how hard I worked to get this gig in Portland? I'd turned Travis down when he asked me to be his photographer so I could take a better paying job in Belize. But after I saw you in Washington, I spent a week convincing him to dump the photographer he'd been talking to and let me work with him. I knew it would be a long assignment in the Northwest and it would give me a chance to see you."

"You turned down more money to come here?"

He kissed the tip of her nose. "Yup, you were worth more. And I've been moving some things around to free up a couple, three weeks so I can come back to Portland after my next two assignments. I have the week in New Mexico, then a week on the ship. Then, after we both have some time apart, maybe we can figure out what this is between us. Are you willing to try?"

She closed her eyes and thought about the weeks they'd spent together, about how easily she'd fallen into wanting him around. About how hard it would be to give him up.

And how much it hurt when Mark betrayed her.

"I won't stop you from coming back to Portland," she said.

He pulled her close. "That's the best I can get tonight, I imagine." He kissed her forehead. She put her arm over his and nestled her head into his shoulder. Eventually, as he rubbed her back and kissed her hair, she began to feel the tension drain out of her body and even to her surprise, after awhile, began to slip slowly into sleep.

• • •

Cold, fully dressed and with Fiona still tangled in his arms, Nick woke at 6 A.M. He'd not only never undressed after he'd soothed her to sleep, but apparently he'd fallen asleep himself before he managed to get under the blanket. He slipped out of bed and took a hot shower as quietly as he could, put on clean boxers, turned up the heat, and went to the kitchen to make coffee.

He had royally fucked up the night before. Why he thought he needed to herd Fiona into some sort of box about their relationship, he didn't know. He had never thought in terms of forever-after with a woman, so why had he been so insistent? Was he really ready to settle in one place, giving up the freedom to take off whenever a good assignment came up for a domestic life?

Or was this fantasy of roots and a family the result of hanging out with his sister for longer than usual, watching her with her family? In spite of wanting to get her off his back most of the time, he'd always admired her and had often walked in her footsteps. When she went off to college to follow her dream of being an artist, it gave him the courage to pursue journalism. When she struck out on her own as a glass artist, it gave him the idea to enlarge his view of what he could do with the images he took other than sell them to magazines and newspapers.

So now, when he saw her settled with the man she loved and who clearly loved her, saw her as the contented mother of a daughter and the stepmother of two sons, was he trailing after her again or was this what he really wanted?

Maybe it would be better to back off a little. Give this some thought while he was away, like he'd said to Fee last night. Then, when he came back to Portland, maybe they could talk about it more intelligently.

Maybe Fee was the one who knew what the smartest course was and he should let her set the pace. He'd better figure it out quickly so he could make it right with her when she woke.

• • •

Nick wasn't there. His pillow was cool to her touch, which meant he'd been out of bed for a while. She hugged it to her, inhaling the smell of him on the pillowcase, a clean smell of soap and his cologne, a smell she would never forget. He was so sweet, so loving, so open. Nothing like her ex. Why was she hesitating about what he'd said last night?

She clutched the pillow, listening for sounds of him in the living room, but the door to the bedroom was closed and she couldn't hear anything. Maybe he'd left. After last night, she wasn't sure she'd blame him if he had. No, his jeans were on the chair across the room, his leather bag beside it.

Wrapping her robe around her, she opened the door and immediately smelled coffee. In the kitchen she found Nick, in boxer shorts and bare feet, putting dishes away in the cabinet. She could see he'd been busy—all the remains of their uncooked, uneaten meal from the night before had been cleaned up and all the dishes washed.

She stood beside the breakfast table, not sure what to say, so she said nothing. When he turned and saw her, a smile curved his mouth and broke her heart.

"Morning, beautiful," he said. "Coffee?"

"Yes, please."

He grabbed two mugs from the counter and poured the fresh brew into them, brought one mug to her and put it on the table before he gathered her into his arms and kissed her. "About last night. I'm sorry. You're right. We need to go as fast as we can go together. So, a day at a time is how we'll do it."

She was vaguely disappointed by his acquiescence. "I'm the one who should be apologizing and asking for another chance."

"Please. It was me being a sweet young thing. We're impatient."

"I thought we'd forgotten my stupid comment."

"I've had second thoughts. I've decided I want to be your sweet young thing. Among other reasons, it gives me something to hide behind every now and then. Like this morning." He went to the other side of the kitchen and got his mug of coffee. "It also gives me a reason to demand breakfast. Sweet young things need to be fed, particularly when they get sent to bed without any dinner."

"Yeah, we both kinda did, didn't we? Let me take a shower and get dressed and I'll make us something to eat." She watched him for a moment, not sure whether to say any more about the night before—but Nick was making it clear he wanted to leave it alone so she would, too. Before she went to the bedroom, she asked, "Are you shooting someplace today?"

"Yeah, Mt. Adams, assuming the weather cooperates."

"I don't like to sound like Amanda, but make sure you have your phone on, will you? And let me know when you're on the way home, please?"

"You do sound like my sister. Why?"

"I don't know. I don't usually believe in premonitions but something feels weird about today."

He came up behind her and put his arm around her waist, nuzzling her neck. "It's probably just an emotional hangover from last night."

"Maybe. But be careful, will you?"

"Nothing's going to happen. But I'll be careful, I promise."

Chapter 13

Lost in unanswerable questions, Nick almost missed the turnoff to Trout Lake and the Mt. Adams highway. Had he panicked Fiona last night? Overplayed his hand? Trapped himself with words he'd never be able to take back? He didn't know. He did know there wasn't much time left to try and make it right. Travis arrived the next day; they would be shooting all over the Cascades for the next week...his alone time with Fiona would be limited.

Lack of time with her was one sure thing. The other one? He was clearly falling for the beautiful redhead. What wasn't clear was what loving her meant, for now or for the future.

A sign for the South Spur trailhead directed him to a place to park his car. And once he started hiking the trail and taking scouting shots of the Gifford Pinchot National Forest for Travis, he got lost in something other than questions—the light, the beauty of the trees, lost in doing the job he loved.

He took image after image of waterfalls and stunning views of Mt. Adams, the creeks and rivers running full and the beginning of the wildflower season. He even got a couple shots of what he thought was a Northern Spotted Owl. The one thing he hadn't seen was another human being. It was a good day.

Then, hours later, when he got back to his car it was apparent he'd been mistaken about the lack of people. There had been at least one other person around.

With a knife.

All four of his tires had been slashed and the note stuffed under the windshield wiper explained why. "If your smart you'll stick to your piktures and stay out of other peoples busness. If you don't, theirs a chance you'll end up like your tires."

Bad grammar and spelling aside, he was sure whoever had written it meant every word.

It took him twenty minutes to find enough cell signal to call Triple A and more than two hours for them to get to him with new tires. Which was just enough time to amp up his fear that the tire-slasher was still around. He jumped at every sound, every tree branch moving in the breeze, every call of a bird, every rustle of dry grass. Usually when he was in a tight place his photographer's eye would divert his attention and he could manage the fear by shooting images. Not today. Even the sight of a doe coming out of the woods with her fawn to eat in the late afternoon light wasn't enough to take his mind off the fact that someone had followed him and threatened his life. This wasn't just a photo shoot. It was personal.

• • •

Fiona fussed all day about the conversation of the night before and her premonition about Nick heading for trouble. Her uneasiness about what was getting to be a dangerous confluence of her personal and professional lives got worse when her contact in the Forest Service added one more bit of information to what she knew—the name of the in-holder who had the rights to the property on Mt. Hood where the cabin stood was Duke Wellington.

Suspicion confirmed.

Or was it? Her contact went on to say he'd sublet it to a corporation—an out-of-state company called Energy, Inc. The company had built the cabin. The Forest Service had seen and approved the plans but had never met anyone other than the attorney representing the company.

Fiona immediately called Wellington's office but he was away on business so she could only leave a message. A half-dozen phone calls and a couple hours of searching online failed to give her any more information about Energy, Inc. Whoever was behind the company was apparently quite good at hiding.

She was just about to get back to worrying about Nick when she got a call from Tyler Radke, chief of staff for City Commissioner Harris Wilson. The commissioner was not the most cordial of sources for Fiona, but his staffer had lately been a reliable contact. Since Wilson routinely voted against the mayor, Radke was a good source on any number of stories, including the Anderbock bill, which his boss supported. The progress of the bill was the reason for Radke's call.

Fiona listened for a while, asked a few questions, and then moved the subject to the attempted assassination.

"Look," Radke said after a pause. "I'm not saying it was a good idea, what he did, but I have to say, trying to take the city in the direction she's advocating, punishing the businesses we need to grow the economy, is bound to raise the hackles of a lot of people."

"Give me some examples of what you think is taking us in the wrong direction."

"It's not me, Fiona. It's my boss. He's concerned about the costs to business to rename streets, mandate longer parental leave, and paid sick days. And don't get me started on her support for increasing the minimum wage or her tax increases for developers."

She noticed Radke had slipped into "me" but didn't mention it. Bringing the conversation back to the attempt on the mayor's life, she said, "But there have been disagreements between mayors and commissioners for the whole history of the city. Why do you think this mayor is such a lightning rod that a man tried to kill her?"

"From what I heard about the man who shot at her, it had to do with race. Not how Commissioner Wilson would want to address his differences with her."

"And how would he do it?"

"The way any of us would. In an election."

"Is your boss running for mayor?"

"Off the record? He's been approached by people to run."

"People?"

"Come on, Fiona, you know how this works. You ask the questions you want answered without giving away any of your sources. I answer by giving you as much information as I want you to have."

She laughed. "So have we reached the end of what you want me to know about this subject?"

"For the moment."

"Thanks, I appreciate your honesty." Before she let him go, she said, "Tyler, two last questions. I'm sure you've heard the rumors about a white supremacist group interested in moving into Portland."

"Yeah," he said, hesitantly. "What've you heard?"

"Not much. Just the name of the organization and the possibility it's backed by the deep pockets of a businessman in town. Any chance you know more?"

"I've heard a couple names. I assume you have, too."

"Who have you heard?"

"Wellington and Cochran. I can't believe either of them would put themselves out there, although you never know." He paused for a moment. "Not that you asked my advice, but you might want to be careful where you're asking questions. Whoever tried to have the mayor shot isn't a nice person."

"I'll keep it in mind."

"What's the other one?"

"Other one?"

"You said you had two questions."

Fiona hesitated. Something about what Radke had said made her slightly uneasy about tipping her hand about the cabin. But it wasn't a big enough red flag to stop her from eventually saying, "I was hiking in the Mt. Hood National Forest recently and came on a cabin with some of the regalia of the group we're talking about. It was built by a group called Energy, Inc. You know anything about the cabin or the group?"

"The group sounds familiar. Let me nose around and see what I can find out. I'll get back to you."

For a few minutes after the call, she sat at her desk and mulled the conversation over in her mind. Odd that he only mentioned two of the four names everyone else mentioned. And he'd given her another warning. It was getting to be a regular thing when she asked questions about the White Knights. After Garland's death and what had happened with Nick's car, she not only didn't like it, she was frightened by it.

On the other hand, Radke had volunteered to help her find information on the cabin. Maybe he was just being a good guy telling her to be careful. Somehow she doubted it.

Just before she left her office, she got a text message from Nick saying he was on his way back to Portland and should be at her house within the hour. She felt a sense of relief when she read it. He was okay. Her premonition was just nerves.

• • •

Nick got to the house, used the key he had to get in, then threw the deadbolt on the door, and immediately went to the front window. Concealing himself behind the curtain, he looked out and scanned the neighborhood.

"Nick? What are you doing? What's going on?" Fiona asked as he dropped the curtain and turned to her.

"Nothing. Everything's fine." He tried to reassure her with a kiss but, not really focusing on what he was doing, he missed her mouth by a couple inches.

"No, seriously, what's up? You're scaring me."

"Do you have a phone number for Sam at work?"

"Yeah, why?"

"Your premonition was on target, so to speak. My tires were all slashed when I got back from shooting and there was a note saying I'd better keep my nose out of other people's business. I need to talk to Sam, but I don't want Amanda to know or she'll freak. I thought I'd try to get him before he left his desk. Where's the number?"

She was frozen in place, fear obvious on her face.

"Fee, the number?" He was losing time and patience and knew it showed in his voice.

"Threatened? Where?" Her voice was choked, probably with the same fear he saw in her expression.

"Near a trailhead on Mt. Adams, where I left my car. It took forever for someone to come with new tires." He ran his hands over his face as if to smooth out the tension lines. "I'm never going to be able to rent from Hertz again, am I?"

"This isn't funny, Nick."

"I know it isn't, Fee, believe me. The only good thing is, whoever did it was clearly out to scare me, not hurt me." He held out his hand again. "Sam's number? Please?"

"Sorry, hold on." She went to the dining room and came back with her phone. "It's in my contacts."

Sam answered, "Hi, Fiona."

"It's Nick."

"Okay, hi, Fiona's phone. What's going on, brother-in-law? Did they get your phone, too, when they bagged your camera?"

"No, but I wanted to call you at work and Fee had your number saved. I have something to tell you I don't want Amanda to know."

"We don't keep things from each other unless there's a damned good reason."

"I think this qualifies." He summarized what happened while he was out shooting.

"You okay?" Sam asked.

"I'm fine. I watched on the way home. No one seemed to be following me. I really don't want Amanda to worry."

"I agree with you. You'll need to make a police report in Washington State but I'll do my best to keep it under wraps here until it's sorted out."

"Thanks, Sam."

"But my price is this: restrict your travels to places where there are other people. Or have people with you."

"My writer will be here in a couple days."

"Not sure you should be going into the woods with just one other person."

"This guy's the perfect companion. He's a big believer in the Second Amendment. He's driving up from Northern California. Probably has a shoulder-fired missile launcher in his trunk. I'll be perfectly safe with him."

"Great. Not only are we outgunned by the bad guys, we're outgunned by the people we're trying to protect. Maybe we should just stockpile RPGs and AK-47s on every block and do away with the cost of maintaining a police force."

Nick could imagine the look on his brother-in-law's face. "I assume you're not looking for a response."

"No, I'm not. How's Fiona taking it?" Sam asked.

"She's hyperventilating; fussing over me."

Sam laughed. "Who needs Amanda? You have Fiona to act in her place. I'd tell her not to worry but I don't think it would work. So just tell her we'll take care of it."

• • •

At Fiona's request, Nick stayed again that night. This time it was so she could feel comfortable about his safety, which helped her sleep until a phone call awakened them both.

"Fiona, get down here right now."

She glanced at the clock—it was six in the morning. What had happened that her boss was calling her at this hour?

"Down where? What's going on?"

"The mayor's been shot. I need you at City Hall, with a camera if you have one other than on your phone. Our errant photographer is missing again."

"I can do better than my old camera. I've got a photojournalist here. I'll bring him."

"Get him here ASAP." Ben Stern didn't wait for her to answer before hanging up.

The drive from St. Johns to downtown was silent. At least inside the car. Inside her head Fiona was trying to beat back the adrenaline-fueled fears that whoever was behind this was escalating things. Death threats, slashed tires, another attempt on the mayor. Maybe she shouldn't have suggested Nick come along. Maybe this would put him more in the line of fire. But it was too late for that. He'd been as excited as she was to get dressed and into the car.

They arrived in downtown Portland to find traffic in the streets leading up to the complex of city, county, and federal buildings at a complete standstill. Police were all over the place, trying to direct traffic and keep people away from the crime scene.

Most of the near-by on-street parking was taken so, risking a rather large ticket, Fiona finally parked—more like abandoned—her car in a loading zone and ran the remaining half-mile to the Fourth Avenue side of City Hall, now festooned with yellow crime scene tape. Fiona looked for her boss but didn't see him. Then she looked for Sam or one of the other police officers she knew but couldn't get anyone's attention even when she did see someone familiar.

She had to wait for Ben Stern to find her about five minutes later.

"What the fuck happened?" she asked.

"The mayor and her chief of security were coming into the building for an early morning meeting. Someone stepped out of the shadows over there," he said, pointing to a group of trees to the north, "and fired six shots. Two hit the mayor before Bud could get between her and the shooter. He took the rest of the rounds."

"Please don't tell me..."

"Okay, I won't. But he is."

"Oh, God. How is she?"

"Don't know. Is this your photographer?" he asked indicating Nick, who was shooting images of chalk outlines and shell casings, blood spatters, police tape, and the officers crawling all over the scene looking for evidence, anything he thought relevant and from all angles.

"Yeah. Nick, meet Ben Stern. Ben, Nick St. Claire."

"If you'll give us an exclusive on those images, we'll pay you," Stern said, looking not at Nick but at where Nick was aiming his camera.

"I'll email them to you as soon as I have access to a computer. Use what you want. Just give me a credit." He turned to Fiona. "How long you gonna be here, Fee? I have to meet Travis out in Troutdale and we're heading up to Mt. Hood from there."

She looked at her boss, who said, "There's a presser in fifteen minutes, then you can get out of here. As soon as you drop him off, get the story on the web, then see what you can find out to make it bigger."

The hastily called press conference was brief. The chief announced little the media didn't already know. The mayor and her security chief had been shot at close range as they entered City Hall. The security chief was pronounced dead on the scene. The mayor had been taken to Oregon Health Sciences University. An update on her condition would be given later in the afternoon at a press conference at OHSU.

No questions were allowed.

After ferrying Nick home to make his dash to meet his buddy, she drove on over to the newspaper office. She tried to wring information out of Sam on the phone, but he didn't know much more other than a few details about the caliber of the bullet. He was as terse and tense sounding as Fiona had ever heard him.

Which wasn't a surprise. She knew the dead security chief had been his friend.

She got a piece about the shootings online and headed back downtown to see what more she could dig out from her contacts in City Hall. This time, in addition to the police barricade, she found a hastily sprung up memorial of flowers, candles, and American flags. There were also two groups of people, one from the mayor's church praying around the memorial, the other, the disgusting one, a picket line of a few men with signs saying the mayor got what was coming to her. And with the swastikas tattooed on their arms, she didn't have to guess why they were blaming her.

From the sidewalk she called a couple contacts inside City Hall. She found out the mayor, who had been wearing a protective vest, had been shot once in the shoulder and once in the abdomen. She was in surgery, but her docs were optimistic about her prognosis.

Fiona also learned this shooter had been either more intelligent than Preston Garland or had planned better. This one had gotten away. It was apparent, however, he—several bystander accounts said it was a man—had help as well as inside information about the mayor's schedule. Only a handful of people knew she would be there so early. The focus of inquiry was on the few people, staff, and city commissioners mainly, who knew about the meeting called to discuss the mayor's proposal to rename Broadway for Abigail Scott Duniway, the woman who'd spearheaded the drive for a woman's right to vote in Oregon.

Fiona worked all her sources but no one could give her much more. The commissioners were tight lipped. The mayor's supporters only wanted to talk about their ideas of who was responsible, none of which had any supporting evidence, and some of which were wild at best. It was one dead-end after another.

But if City Hall contacts didn't have much to say, others did. The whole city was out on a ledge where a gust of rumor could blow them off. The Police Bureau had dozens of tips on the Bureau hotline as well as demands from all sides, ranging from people on the street to TV and radio talking heads to solve it.

After a good hour of chasing smoke, Fiona got a phone call from Tyler Radke asking her to meet him in an hour at a coffee cart two blocks from City Hall so they could talk.

Normally, she wasn't uncomfortable about meeting sources in a public place. But the events of the morning made her distinctly uneasy. So she reported in to her boss, telling him where she was going, who she was meeting, and promising to keep Stern posted.

Tyler seemed nervous when she met up with him. *Good,* she thought. *That makes two of us.*

"I don't have a lot of time," he said, looking over his shoulder in the direction of City Hall. "Everyone's watching everyone else so I don't want to be seen talking to you for too long. You asked about a cabin on Mt. Hood. I overheard Commissioner Daystrom talking to his staffer, saying they needed to stay away from the Mt. Hood cabin until this blew over to protect the White Knights. The staffer said he'd get an email out to everyone. Said it had been cleaned out and no one needed to be there anyway."

"Daystrom? Wow. He's not the most progressive person in the city, but I wouldn't have thought he'd be mixed up in something like this. Not with his strong religious stand on how we're all God's children."

"You have any contacts with his office?"

"No one there is usually interested in talking to me."

"I'll see what I can do to find someone for you."

"Thanks, Tyler, appreciate it."

"What do you think you'll do?"

The uneasiness about talking to Tyler was back. Her gut told her not to be too forthcoming about her plans. "I don't know yet. I'll have to think about it."

"You seemed interested in the place the last time we talked. I thought maybe if the cabin was deserted for a while, you could go have a look."

"I may. I had to leave quickly the last time. Like I said, I'll think about it."

"It may give you the answers you're looking for. But be careful. Wouldn't want you to get hurt because of something I told you."

As she walked away she replayed the conversation in her mind. There was something off about it, but damned if she knew what it was.

Chapter 14

"No, Fiona, you're not going up on the mountain alone." Stern was adamant.

"Then you come with me," she said to her boss. "I want to take another look at the cabin. It's important. I know it is. I can feel it."

"I respect your instincts, but I'm concerned about your safety. And I can't go. I have an editorial meeting and someone has to ride herd on the City Hall shooting story if you're off chasing White Knights."

"It's all connected. I'm telling you. And with everyone's attention here, it's the perfect time to see what the hell's going on up *there*." She waved in the general direction of the mountain.

Stern closed his eyes and seemed to be mulling it over. "How about your friend Nick? Didn't he say he and his writer were going up to Mt. Hood today?"

"I've been trying to get in touch with him. Texted him to meet me at the cabin. But I haven't heard back from him."

"Try again. I want someone with you." Stern started to walk away from her desk. "And let someone in law enforcement know what's going on. It sounds like the cabin's in the Clackamas County part of Mt. Hood. Which is good. They might not be off looking for the City Hall shooter the way everyone here is. Call them."

"I will. I promise. And for good measure I'll call Sam Richardson. He's been talking to me on background about this."

She kept her promise. At least most of it. She called the Clackamas County sheriff's office, told a bored receptionist what she was doing, how it was connected with the events on Portland, and then called Sam at his desk and left a message. And she texted Nick again.

But when he still hadn't answered fifteen minutes later, she left the office and headed east for Mt. Hood, figuring by the time she got to the cabin, she'd have contact with him.

She parked in the same spot where they'd left the car on their last excursion, wrote a note about where she was to leave on the driver's seat and texted Nick again. Then she waited. Ten minutes turned to fifteen. Then twenty. There was not a living soul around. Other than bugs buzzing and birds chirping, it was as still and silent as the forest could be.

One more text. Nothing. Nick was MIA. Probably out of range of a cell phone tower. Hanging around waiting was absurd. No one was here—Tyler Radke had been sure they'd been warned off. She'd just circle the house, look in the windows, check out the shed she'd seen when she was here before, then leave. Easy-peasy.

The hike into the cabin this time was a lot faster than the hike out had been when she was hopping. But the cabin was no less deserted. She looked in all the windows, seeing little she hadn't noticed before, although she thought some of the flags and tables had been moved around, as if someone—or several someones—had been there.

Going from window to window, she made her way around the cabin until she was at the shed she'd noticed but not investigated before. She tried the door. It wasn't locked this time.

Considering what she found, it was strange it had been left open. Inside was a collection of things she would have figured the owners of the cabin would want to keep secret. On shelves on one side were weapons of all sorts—military style automatic weapons, pistols, nasty-looking knives. Crates of what she took to be ammunition lined the floor under the shelves.

Piled in the back were dozens and dozens—maybe hundreds—of Mayor Carter's campaign signs, many ripped and shredded. Puzzled, she stared at the pile until a conversation she'd had with a Carter campaign staffer came to mind. She'd been complaining about an unusually large number of lost or stolen lawn signs. Fiona hadn't taken her seriously. She should have. Here they were.

There were also poster-size photographs of the mayor, some of them with targets on her face, many of them with bullet holes in them. Fiona finally realized what the chewed up tree and the black and white poster in the cabin were about—Mayor Carter's photograph had been used as target practice. Now she realized what had been nagging at her since the day she and Nick had been there. This was the place where the City Hall shooters practiced.

More shelves on the other wall held boxes with labels on them marked with poison symbols. She didn't recognize the names of some of the chemicals, but she knew how close the cabin was to the source of Portland's water supply, the Bull Run River. The watershed was heavily protected, but still…

She pulled out her phone and was taking shots of everything in the shed when the light from outside was suddenly dimmed and she heard a male voice say, "So, you showed up. We were told you might be here."

Whirling around, she saw three young men with shaved heads blocking the doorway. They were dressed in jeans and T-shirts, which did little to hide their heavily muscled arms and shoulders. They looked to be in their twenties and all three were tattooed with the symbols of the White Power Knights.

Before she could say or do anything, two of them stepped inside the shed. One man grabbed her and dragged her out into the open; another grabbed her phone and smashed it with the butt of the weapon he was carrying.

The third man stood with his arms folded across his chest. "We're supposed to find out what you know and who you've told before we find a permanent cure for your nosy trespassing habits. Pretty thing like you should be fun to play with while we get the job done."

...

"Oh, hell, Trav. You didn't." Nick was retrieving his cameras from the trunk of his friend's car when he came across what he'd been afraid he'd find.

His writer buddy looked over his shoulder, pulled out a handgun, and checked to make sure the safety was still on. "You know I never go anyplace without a weapon. Why are you surprised?"

"I had hopes crossing state lines would deter you."

"Nope. We might need it. Lots of varmints out here in the wilderness."

"A developed campsite near a manmade lake is hardly wilderness." Nick knew he was fighting a losing battle so he grabbed the rest of his gear and shut his mouth and the trunk. "The last time we were up here we were looking for Lava Lake. I think I know how to access it this time. Got a GPS coordinate." He pulled out his iPhone. "Shit. No signal." He pointed to the left. "But I'm pretty sure it's over there."

"Then let's go, bro." Travis clapped Nick on the shoulder and they followed the trail half a mile. There it was—the lake Nick and Fiona had been unable to find.

When he'd gotten photos of the lake from various angles, Nick said, "There's a really interesting cabin somewhere around here. We…I…found when we…I…was here before. Want to take a look?"

Travis grinned. "From the number of times you've said 'we' today, I guess the whole woman-thing has been worth giving up the gig in the Bahamas to come here with me."

"Belize, not the Bahamas. And, yeah, it's been okay." He didn't say any more.

"But that's all the intel I'm getting?"

"Not much else to say. She's beautiful. She's sexy. It's been a great couple of weeks. I'm off to New Mexico next week." He stowed his camera in his bag. "You want to go find the cabin or not?"

Travis stared at him for a few minutes, an amused look on his face. "We getting too close to the flame, are we? Getting burned?"

"Go fuck yourself, Trav. I'm heading for the cabin. You coming?"

Travis grunted a laugh and checked to make sure his gun was still in its holster. "Will it work for my story?"

"Doubtful. It's some sort of white power camp. Fiona's working on a story about it."

"So her name's Fiona. She even sounds sexy and beautiful."

Nick strode off on the trail toward the cabin without rising to the bait. Ten minutes later the two men approached the cabin from the rear. Nick started to explain to his colleague how he and Fiona had stumbled on the cabin while looking for Lava Lake.

"We came up the trail from the other direction. It was…"

He was interrupted by a scream. The two men stopped.

"What the hell?" Travis asked. "That sounded like a woman."

Then they heard the rough sounds of male voices, several of them.

"Shut up, bitch," one said.

"No one'll hear you anyway," another said.

"Let me go," the woman said. A very familiar woman—Fiona.

Nick's heart rate jumped. His breath got shallow. He motioned Travis back into the shadow of a grove of trees.

"Fuck, she bit me," a male voice said.

"I'll do worse than bite you if you don't let me go," Fiona said, her voice sounding less brave than her words did.

Nick explained who the woman was.

"It sounds like there's more than one man there, too," Travis said.

"But there are two of us. Let's go get her," Nick said.

"No, she'll get hurt. We need the police." Travis was waving his cell phone around, searching for a signal. When he shook his head indicating his failure, Nick tried, found a weak one and called Sam, quickly explaining what was happening.

Sam sounded as angry as Nick had ever heard him. "What the hell are you doing up on the mountain? And why are you calling me? You're in Clackamas County. I told you both..." He disappeared into the crackle of lost signal.

Nick moved to another place where he could hear the end of Sam's rant and whispered, "Sorry I haven't memorized the county boundaries in the state of Oregon, Sam, but..."

"I'll call the sheriff and head up there myself. Let us handle it. Don't interfere. I don't want you or your friend to get involved."

"Fiona's in danger."

"Did you hear me? Stay away. Now, get off the damn phone and let me get the sheriff."

Nick got off the phone as ordered but if he didn't hear police sirens in the next few minutes no way in hell was he going to stay away from the scene in front of the cabin.

He and Travis crept around from behind the cabin, listening the whole time to the sounds of Fiona and the men tormenting her. When they finally got to a place where they could see what was going on, it was enough to make Nick want to ignore what Sam said and try to get to Fiona—whatever the risk. Three muscular, young men with weapons tucked into the back of their jeans were toying with Fiona like a pack of wild animals with a frightened prey.

Nick had been in tight circumstances before when he covered international hot spots. He'd been shot at, held at knifepoint, once even captured and held for a couple days by some teenage rebels who turned out to be nice kids. Nothing, however, including the threat he'd gotten from the tire-slasher, had scared him more than the sound of Fiona's voice quivering with fear.

Two of them had her in the middle of a big piece of cloth—a flag it looked like—pitching her up and down. They'd stop, the third man would slap her, ask her a question about what she knew, who she'd talked to, taunt her, then let his buddies toss her around again, throwing her higher in the air with each pass. She was mouthing off to them, which seemed to amuse them although the amusement seemed to be wearing thin as he and Travis listened.

The look on her face confirmed what Nick had heard in her voice—she was terrified in spite of her defiant words. He couldn't bear to see her tormented like that, but he couldn't look away. What he saw only amped up his frustration. The woman he had fallen in love with was in danger and he was standing around like a little kid waiting for daddy to arrive and rescue them both.

The men seemed in no hurry to do anything more violent than pass her around for the fun of it, so Nick allowed his friend to restrain him from roaring into the scene. Travis had taken the safety off his weapon and Nick wanted nothing more than to grab the gun from Travis and charge the clearing like Lancelot rescuing Guinevere from being incinerated. But he'd promised Sam he'd wait for the cops.

Instead of the sound of law enforcement arriving, however, all they heard were the sounds of the skinheads tormenting Fiona. Nick tried to calm himself; tried to keep his anger in check. It wasn't working.

Then the scene in front of them changed. Seeming to tire of their sport, the skinheads dumped Fiona on the ground, the two who'd been throwing her in the air picked her up, held her by her arms as still as they could, while the third one took a knife from his boot and asked again who she had told about the cabin. When she refused to answer, he cut off the top button on her shirt. He repeated the question. She shook her head. The second button went and he slapped her. By the time the third button was gone and she'd been hit again, Nick lost it. He motioned to Travis to follow him and made a run at the skinheads.

It was not his best move of the day. The skinheads had the advantages of being younger and more muscular than either Travis or Nick. While the one with a knife held onto Fiona, one took on Travis, kicking his weapon out of his hand before throwing a punch at him and the third one came straight for Nick.

All Nick could see was a huge guy with more muscles that Schwarzenegger and a stance that said he'd been in more fights than Nick had. Which wasn't hard because Nick had never been in a fight. But he wasn't going down without trying.

He swung at the guy and missed, getting a fist in the nose in return that made him see stars. Blindly, blood dripping down the back of this throat and over his mouth he threw another punch. It landed hard enough in the skinhead's gut to slow him down for a few seconds, long enough for Nick to try and land another blow, but his opponent was faster. He tried to defend himself, to get in another blow, but the hits to his body came hard and fast. There was no way he could make any headway on fighting off the kid who was beating him into submission, first with his fists then, when he had Nick on the ground, with his feet.

He could hear Fiona screaming his name, heard Travis grunt as the second guy beat on him. Neither was the sound he wanted to hear.

Then there it was—the sweet sound of police sirens. He tried to grab the feet of the man who was kicking him, to hold him for the cops, but he was unable to get a grip on him as the guy took off for the trees, yelling, "Run."

"Do you have her phone?" the man who'd been fighting with Travis asked.

"Fuck the phone. Get the hell out of Dodge," the one who'd been holding Fiona said.

Nick sat up, painfully and slowly. Through eyes beginning to swell, he saw Travis, who somehow looked unharmed from the fight he'd been in, pick up his gun from the ground, stand, aim and fire four shots at the retreating figures. One of the three men fell, shot in the leg from the look of it. A second man grabbed an arm, as if hit, then tripped and fell hard, where he lay not moving. The third man disappeared into the forest.

Barely able to move without hurting in places he had hitherto not known existed, Nick wiped blood out of his eyes, and tried to find Fiona. He didn't have to look far. She was right next to him.

"Oh, God, Nick. Can you get up?" She looked more terrified now than she had when she'd been at the mercy of the skinheads. "This is all my fault. If I hadn't texted you..." She began to cry as she wiped at the blood he could feel coming out of his nose with the sleeve of her shirt.

"Text? What text?" he started but was interrupted by the entrance of an Oregon state trooper, then by a Clackamas County sheriff's deputy, last by an EMT. It was semi-organized chaos as more cops arrived and the two wounded skinheads were cuffed, Travis was taken to a police vehicle to talk to the sheriff's deputy, and Fiona was tended to by an EMT.

And then there was Sam, who'd also shown up. He had no actual jurisdiction, but it didn't prevent him from yelling—loudly enough to be heard in Portland—about what a jackass Nick been to tackle the skinheads by himself. Before Nick could defend his actions, he, too, was hustled away to have his injuries looked at by the medics while the troopers talked to him.

He tried to explain he needed to talk to Fiona but he was blocked at every turn by some law enforcement official or other who wanted to hear what he had to say. The only thing comforting him was the fact that when he patted down his pockets, he was relieved to find he still had his cell. When they finished with him, he'd call her.

He'd deal with Sam later, too.

• • •

"What the fuck were you doing here, Fiona?" Sam Richardson was clearly not in the mood to be civil.

She'd finished talking to one set of cops and was waiting to talk to the sheriff's deputy when he grabbed her. "My job, like I told you. What're you doing here? Isn't this out of your jurisdiction?"

"I told you to stay away from here. These guys are dangerous. As you have only too fucking recently found out."

"You didn't tell me any such thing. And I had no intention of meeting up with them. I heard the place was deserted. I figured with everyone in the Portland metro area looking for the City Hall shooter, I might have a chance to see what was up here."

"Instead you put yourself and Nick in danger."

She closed her eyes for a moment, seeing the blood all over Nick's face. "Is he all right? I couldn't get near him to find out after the police and EMTs got here."

"From the blood I'd say there's not a chance in hell he's all right. But that must not be important to you. Getting your story is more important, isn't it?"

"What a terrible thing to say, Sam."

"The truth sometimes is." He rubbed his hands over his face. "Christ, how'm I going to tell Amanda you caused her brother to be hauled off bleeding all over the place?"

"I didn't ask Nick to come charging into the middle of a pack of wild animals."

He glared at her, as if to say, "You didn't have to ask."

"Look, Sam, I found out who owned this cabin and came up here to see what else I could discover for my story."

"Your story. Your damned story is all that matters to you, isn't it?"

"It's my job. Of course it matters. Doesn't your job matter to you?"

He shook his head. "My job is to keep people out of danger, whereas yours seems to be—"

"Fuck off, Sam. I'm finished with this conversation." Fiona stomped away to be waylaid by the Clackamas County Sheriff's department contingent. She promised to meet them in Oregon City in two hours and headed for her car, furious Sam hadn't even once asked how she was. How dare he blame her for everything when the other cops seemed to accept she was the victim not the villain.

Yet she was furious at herself, too. Mostly for getting the man she loved into the middle of something she'd likely be having nightmares about for the rest of her life. Because in spite of her indignation at how Sam treated her, she was beginning to believe he was right—because she wanted her story, she had gotten Nick badly injured.

She barely remembered driving down the mountain to her house, changing her clothes, and heading south to Oregon City. All she remembered for days afterward, other than flashbacks of the fear she'd felt when she thought the skinheads really were going to kill her, was the growing sense of guilt about how she had demanded Nick come meet her at the cabin only to have him leave bloodied, battered, and beaten.

How could she ever face him again?

Chapter 15

For the next few days, Fiona stayed home and out of sight. She went out only to deal with more police and to make sure her doctor was satisfied she had no internal injuries. She stayed out of the way of her colleagues in the press. She had a newfound sympathy for people whose lives had been thrown into chaos by some horrific event only to find themselves the object of journalists who wanted them to endlessly relive it. All the victims wanted to do was forget.

And because her guilt about what happened to Nick grew every time she read about the man "badly beaten" as the reports kept saying, she also spent the time avoiding phone calls from Nick, Amanda, and Margo, too embarrassed to talk to any of them. Because of her, Nick had been hurt. Not only could she not face him, she had to avoid her friends, too.

When she did go back to work, her boss kept telling her she'd done everything she should have done to protect herself—notified the right people, kept in touch with her office, even left a note in the car.

And, he pointed out, her instinct to run down the story about the White Power Knights by looking at the cabin again had been a good one. When the police searched the place, they found a gold mine of information on the shady organization and the money behind it. Once the lid had been torn off the story, everything unraveled quickly.

The only thing she could do to forget was to follow her story. In a phone call she made to get his take on what happened, Duke Wellington said he had, indeed, leased the property where the cabin was located. But he'd sublet it to a group headed by Sherman Bischler, supposedly for a summer camp for teenagers, when

Wellington's plans for a second home for his family changed. He'd never been up to see what Bisch had done with the land.

And from a friendly source in City Hall she confirmed what she'd already suspected—Tyler Radke had been feeding misinformation to staffers and reporters alike for months trying to keep suspicion away from himself and the man who was paying him to be the eyes and ears of the White Knights—not the city commissioner he worked for, but Sherman Bischler.

Radke was currently in police custody after one of the passersby outside City Hall on the morning of the second shooting identified him as the man who whisked away the shooter in his car. When the security tape from the day of the first assassination attempt was reviewed again, it was Tyler Radke who was seen avoiding the metal detector and someone who looked a lot like him herding Preston Garland out the door after his attempt on the mayor's life.

The second assassin was still at large, but they had a description and a huge reward posted by Duke Wellington, which had generated hundreds of tips.

Finally, when her best attempts to avoid being part of the story instead of just writing it failed, Fiona asked the law enforcement officials on the case if she could stay with her parents in Tacoma for a couple weeks. They agreed. She left Portland without talking to any of her friends, hoping she would find at her parents' house a place to write her stories in peace and maybe find a way to manage her guilt.

• • •

"Nick, would you take some of this cake with you?" Amanda had a cake knife in one hand and a paper plate in the other.

It was bad enough he had presents to take with him reminding him of his Fiona-less birthday. The last thing he needed was cake.

"I loved it, Sis, but I don't think it'll survive in my carry-on," Nick said.

"Tony?"

"Don't you dare," Margo said. "I'll eat it if we take it home, and I've already had two pieces. I have absolutely no resistance to chocolate."

Sam took the knife and plate from his wife. "Here, I'll take some of it to work tomorrow and eliminate the problem." He cut a large slab of cake and put it on the plate.

"Put it out for the others, Sam. You've already had…"

"Nick, are you sure you have to leave? When you're here my wife splits her hovering between the two of us, but when you're not here, I get the brunt of it," Sam said.

"You signed up for it, Sam. I was just born into it. Can't stay. Have to go teach all those people who signed up to learn from a famous photojournalist how to get more out of their cameras," he said.

"At last you'll have a chance to put all the experience you got teaching Mom how to use her various cameras," Amanda said.

"I doubt anyone who signed up for these classes is so camera illiterate. And if you ever tell Mom what I said, your husband will be arresting his brother-in-law for the murder of his wife," he said.

"I better get going. I have to pack all these goodies you gave me." He kissed his sister and gave her a hug. "Thanks for a great birthday dinner, Amanda, and for the Kindle gift cards. Tell Kat again how much I love her pictures when she wakes up tomorrow, especially the one of Chihuly. I think we've discovered the next generation artist in the family."

He clapped his brother-in-law on the back in a guy hug, did the same with Tony, and then kissed Margo on the cheek. "Thank you for the DVDs, you two. They'll be a great distraction on the plane flight."

"Fly safe, Nick," Margo said.

"When will we see you again?" Amanda asked.

"Not sure. I have these two photo instruction gigs, then I have to work out my schedule. I thought I'd be coming...never mind. I'll let you know."

Amanda put her arm around her brother as she walked him to the door. "Have you called her?" she said in a quiet voice.

"Not in the past couple days."

"Don't you think...?"

"I think when someone doesn't return a dozen text messages, even more phone calls at work, at home, and on her cell and won't answer my emails, she doesn't want to talk to me."

Sam had followed them and chimed in. "I tried calling her at work, to apologize, but everyone at the paper's covering for her. Couldn't get through the wall they've got around her. I feel bad about this, Nick. Most of the reason she's avoiding you is what *I* said to her."

"It's not your fault."

"Nick," his sister put her hand on his cheek, "I'm worried about you."

"I'm okay, Amanda. I really am. Things didn't work out the way I wanted them to. It happens." Nick walked to the door. "Thanks again. It was a great birthday. I'll call you when I get back from my second trip and let you know I arrived."

When he got to his rental car he sat with his hands on the steering wheel, not starting the car, just staring out the windshield. He wasn't sure he believed what he said back there. But maybe he did. Maybe the truth was, what had happened was for the best. Maybe he was doing what he always did—leaving town when it got complicated with a woman and burying himself in another assignment. It had always worked before. It would work again this time.

Wouldn't it?

Chapter 16

Fiona spent two weeks in Tacoma, finishing up her White Knights series, laying a ghost to rest, and investigating the possibility of a new job where she could maybe do her work differently. But she knew, no matter what she accomplished staying with her parents, nothing would be settled until she went home to Portland and dealt with the past. So she went home to her house in St. Johns, to dusty furniture, a cat that was happy to be out of kitty day care, and fences that needed mending.

She unpacked, started a load of laundry, donned old sweats, took a deep breath, and picked up her phone to make the first difficult call. If she was lucky, she'd get voicemail.

But Amanda answered on the second ring.

"Hi," Fiona started. "Any chance you'll talk to me?"

"Oh, God, girlfriend. I'm so glad to hear from you. I've been pulling my hair out trying to find out where you were."

"I've been with my parents, sorting things out, returning an old robe." She took another deep breath. "I owe you a big apology. I should never have…"

"Returning what? Never mind. No apology needed. After what my husband said to you, you're the one who's owed an apology."

"He was right. I was…"

"You were doing your job. Just the way I'd expect you to."

Fiona could hear voices in the background, calling to Amanda. "I'm sorry. I should have asked if this was a good time. Sounds like I'm interrupting something."

"I have some people here, a new board I'm on. We're having lunch."

"You should have told me. Why don't I call you back?"

"I'll call you. Have you talked to Nick?"

Fiona could feel her eyes fill with tears. "I think that bridge was burned even more thoroughly than any other."

"I don't think so. But we'll talk about it later. I'll call as soon as I get through with this meeting."

Thinking about Nick was not a good thing, so she put music on and set about cleaning with a vengeance to take her mind off him. Several hours later she turned off the vacuum just as Simon and Garfunkel finished accompanying her in singing "I Am a Rock." In the sudden quiet a pounding on the front door startled her. Sure it must be a neighbor with some emergency, she ran to the door saying "What's wrong?" as she opened it.

It wasn't a neighbor. Nick was on the other side of the door looking crisp and neat in tan trousers and a beige and white striped shirt. He was still clean-shaven and still smelled like heaven, if heaven smells like spice cake. She wiped her hand on the side of her sweatpants to get some of the dirt off, then realized she probably wouldn't be shaking hands with him.

"I tried the doorbell but you didn't answer," he said. "I knew you were here because I could hear your music."

"Nick. Hello…what are you…did Amanda call you?"

"Amanda? No, I haven't talked to her since I got off the cruise ship. I came to talk to you. Can I come in?"

"It's not really convenient."

"Please. For a few minutes." He touched her arm.

She recoiled. "I don't have anything to say to you."

"Well, I have things to say to you. And I'd rather not say them out here on your doorstep with all your neighbors walking by."

Over his shoulder she could see the couple from down the street slowly walking their Cock-a-poo past the house, staring at her front door. Right behind them was the woman from across the street with her grandson in a stroller. She, too, was looking at Fiona's house. It seemed like everyone on the block had seen or heard Nick pounding on the door. They all waved when they realized she'd seen them and she waved back.

"Okay, for a few minutes. I'm in the middle of…of stuff." She walked into the living room, where she stood avoiding his eyes, her back straight and her shoulders set, not offering him a seat or taking one herself.

He glanced around the room. "You've moved the furniture around."

She didn't respond. She wasn't about to tell him she was trying to find a way to stop seeing him every place she looked in her house.

He picked up the *Willamette Week* edition with her last White Knights story featured prominently on the cover and flipped through it. "I read all your White Knights stories online. You won't need a cat named Pulitzer after these stories; you'll have the real thing."

"Thanks."

The thump of the newspaper dropping back onto the table was followed by a long awkward silence.

He cleared his throat. "The…ah…'For Rent' sign out front… are you moving? I thought you loved this house."

"I do. But…" She stopped, shook her head and continued, "It's time to move on."

"Where are you going?"

"I have a job offer in Seattle with a start-up online site modeled on *Politico* I'm considering."

"You'd leave *Willamette Week*?"

"Nick, what do you want?"

"Can we sit down? It would be more comfortable, wouldn't it, to sit while we talk?"

"I'm not interested in comfort, thanks. And I told you, I don't have anything to say."

"I do. You didn't give me a chance to say it before I left. Hell, you haven't given anyone a chance to say anything ever since we were in the middle of a crime scene and my brother-in-law was yelling at both of us."

"Right. Because I…" She could feel herself begin to tear up. "You can't just push your way in here like some intruder and then not leave when I ask you to. I'll call the—"

"The police? I can outrank you on that call." He sat on the couch. "Look, you might as well sit down and listen. I'm here until I've said what I came to say. When I'm finished, if you still want me to leave, I will."

Eyes closed, head bowed, she thought about how hard it had been for her to come to terms with what had happened on the mountain and how scared she was he could bring it all back. But she also knew she owed him at least the courtesy to listen to what he had to say. After a long moment she gave in. "All right, have your say and then leave."

He indicated with a gesture for her to sit next to him. Instead she went to the rocking chair across the room. Moving to the edge of the sofa cushion, he leaned forward, his forearms on his thighs, and watched her intently as he said, "When we were on Mt. Hood…"

"We're not going there." Her tone was as defiant as she could make it.

"Yeah, we are. But if you don't want to go there first, I'll start with something easier. I've missed you. I told you before everything blew up I thought we had something special. I haven't changed my mind."

Dismissing his words with a wave of her hand, she said, "It's irrelevant now."

Another long silence followed.

From the tension in his shoulders and the frown on his face, her refusal to engage seemed to be frustrating him, but he sat back on the couch and looked at the ceiling for a moment before saying, "Since you don't want to warm up with the easy stuff, let's get to the hard stuff then." He lowered his gaze and tried to catch her eyes. "What happened on Mt. Hood wasn't your fault. You've been punishing yourself and all the rest of us ever since because you think it was." His look dared her to contradict him.

She didn't. She didn't say anything at all.

"Fiona, did you hear me? I said…"

"What you said is bullshit. It was made perfectly clear to me whose fault it was." She looked down, feeling tears beginning to form again, wanting desperately not to cry in front of him, not sure she could hold it back. Her hands were folded on top of her knees, which were glued together like a well-behaved schoolgirl as she dug her fingernail into the pad of her thumb, trying to concentrate on the pain to keep from crying.

"What got me into trouble was ignoring Sam's instructions, not anything you did. If you'd talk to Sam or me, we'd tell you," Nick said.

"Oh, good. Just what I need, more dissection of what I did. Here's what I know: if I hadn't let my…what did you call it? My passion for a story? If I hadn't let it drive me up the mountain, you'd have never been used as a punching bag by those skinheads." She stopped to wipe at the tears now flowing freely down both cheeks.

"How do you think it felt when Sam accused me of getting you seriously hurt? When he asked me if I realized how upset Amanda would be?" She took several shuddery breaths to get the tears under control. "The worst part…the very worst part…is I had to admit to myself who I am."

Finally, she looked straight into his eyes and said, "I wanted the story. I went up there to get it and you got beat up because of it. That's who I am—a person who would sacrifice the man she…sacrifice another person to get a story. So between guilt piled so high I can barely see over it and realizing my job trumps everything else in my life—which probably makes me not a very good person—it hasn't been…"

She stopped talking and stood up again. "What difference does it make? If you came here to make me feel bad by bringing it all up again, you've accomplished your goal. I'm sure it'll make me a better person to have rehashed it for the millionth time." She started for the door.

Nick rose and grabbed her arm. "I'm not finished. What Sam told me afterward, when he'd looked at things with a clear head, changed everything."

She stared at his hand on her arm so intently he removed it. "It's time for you to leave," she said. "You've run out of the few minutes I had to listen to you."

"You're sure you're not curious about what Sam said?"

"It can't change anything so, no, I'm not."

He looked long and hard at her face. She willed the tears to stop as she held his gaze with a look as fierce as she could make it. Finally, he sighed and said, "Okay, if you've made up your mind. I don't know what else to do." He walked to the door. "This isn't how I wanted things to turn out."

"I'm sorry to disappoint you."

His hand was on the doorknob. He waited a few seconds before turning it, as if he had more to say. Then he turned it and pulled the door open. "Disappointed hardly begins to cover what I feel."

Chapter 17

She fell back against the door after he closed it, torn between relief he'd left and misery he wasn't still in the room where she could smell his aftershave; touch him. God, she wished she'd touched his face just once while he was there, his sweet, handsome face. The memory of how his mouth tasted washed over her. Damn it, why did he have to show up just when she thought she was getting over him?

With the sleeve of her sweatshirt she wiped away the tears leaking from her eyes. As soon as she heard his car pull away, she'd start getting over him—again. Start all over forgetting how much she loved him—because she did love him. Had loved him for a long time now. But it didn't do her any good to finally admit it. She didn't see any future for them. Not after what she'd done.

She realized she'd heard no car door slam. No sound of an engine starting up. Hadn't he left yet? What was he doing out there? Waiting for her to come out? Did he think she'd chase after him?

And what had he meant, Sam had said something to change things? How could words change what happened? She already knew the story. She'd written thousands of words about it. What else was there to know?

Still no sound of a car driving away. Had she missed it because she was crying? She opened the door a crack and saw an unfamiliar car at the curb, but there was no sign of Nick. When she fully opened it, she found him leaning against the railing around the small porch in front of her door.

He straightened, brushed off the seat of his pants, and walked over to her. "I figured your curiosity would work in my favor. It was the part about changing the story, wasn't it?" His expression was hopeful.

"I only came out to make sure you were gone."

"Seriously? You don't want to know what Sam said?"

"Absolutely not." She stood in the doorway with her arms crossed over her breasts, an Amazon guarding her domain, an image somewhat undermined by Pulitzer rubbing up against her ankles and purring.

"Well, then, I guess you do want me to go. So I will." He went down the steps and out toward the curb.

"Wait, Nick. Maybe…"

He stopped but didn't turn around. "You're going to have to tell me what you want, Fee. I'm kinda at a loss here."

"I'm not sure I know either."

He was back on the porch in a few strides, not giving her a chance to change her mind again. "Let's figure it out together. Do we have the same conversation about doing it in front of your neighbors or will you let me in this time without the discussion?"

Saying nothing more, she moved from the doorway and he came back into the house. When they got to the living room he took a handkerchief out of his trouser pocket and began to blot the remains of her tears. The feel of his hands on her face, the tender way he wiped the tears away, made her want to rest her head on his chest so he could wrap her in his arms. She pushed him away before she could act on the thought and went to the bathroom for a tissue. After she splashed water on her face, she blew her nose and returned to the living room.

He was sitting with his left arm along the back of the couch, one ankle resting across the opposite knee. He stretched out his hand to get her to sit next to him. Instead she sat as far away from him on the couch as she could.

"Okay. Let's figure out what you want, Fee."

She shrugged her shoulders but didn't say anything.

"I can't read your mind. You have to tell me."

With a gesture of acquiescence, she gave in. "All right, Nick, you win. I want to know what Sam said."

"Should have started with Sam, shouldn't I? My journalism profs would be so disappointed I buried the lede. They taught me better." He was grinning, more relaxed now than he'd been before.

She glared at him.

"Okay." He held up his hands in surrender. "So, Sam. First, he's been kicking himself from here to hell and gone for what he said to you on the mountain. He apologizes to me every time I talk to him. He's sure you disappeared because of him. Although, come to think of it, I like having him in debt to me this way." He paused, as if giving her a chance to smile or laugh, but she didn't react.

He went on. "He started calling you the next day to tell you, but you wouldn't…"

"To tell me what, Nick? Get to the point."

"That it wasn't your fault. When he saw me, all he could think was he'd catch hell from Amanda because I looked pretty banged up. He lost his temper. But when he talked to your editor the morning after it happened, he discovered you'd done everything the right way. Ben said you told people at work where you were going and when to expect you back in case there was trouble, checked in every hour by phone, only went back up on the mountain when you had been assured by your source the cabin was unoccupied." He took her hand and held it, warding off her attempts to shake him off.

"You tried to get me to meet you there so you weren't alone, notified the sheriff's office, even called Sam, for God's sake, and told him what you were doing. He just didn't get the message until he got back to his desk. Sam knew then he had to apologize for what he said in the heat of the moment, but he hasn't been able to talk to you."

"So he thinks I did things the right way. BFD. How does anything change what happened to you?"

"Let me finish. I, on the other hand, was given a set of specific instructions about what I was to do until the police got there and I violated every one of them. I did myself in, not you."

"You wouldn't have been there if it hadn't been for me."

"I wouldn't have been there if I hadn't been taking photos with Travis."

She managed to free her hand and pulled away from him. "You were at the cabin because you got my texts."

"We were at the cabin because we were on the other side of it photographing Lava Lake. You were right, by the way. The lake isn't very far from the cabin, maybe half a mile. You and I just came at it from a different direction than Travis and I did."

"You didn't get my texts?"

"I didn't know you were there until I heard your voice. I recognized the area when we were shooting and wanted to show Travis the cabin. When I heard you and saw the skinheads roughing you up, I called Sam. He gave me hell for calling him first and not 9-1-1. It was the first thing I did wrong. It wasn't the last.

"He told me to stay out of sight and keep quiet until he or the Clackamas County sheriff got there. I think his biggest concern was Travis. He knew he had a weapon and was afraid he'd use it. It didn't occur to him I'd be the one who'd play cowboy."

"Why did you?"

"You looked terrified. I wanted to be the one who rescued you. They were hurting you. I thought the cops were taking too long. Take your pick. Hell, pick them all."

Finally, she reached for him, tentatively touching his face. He covered her hand with his and kissed her palm. "God, I've missed the feel of you."

Realizing her mistake, she pulled her hand away and stood up to get away from him. "No, I won't let you get around me. How my skin or your mouth feels doesn't change anything."

"My mouth?" He smiled at her. "What about my mouth?"

"Nothing. It doesn't matter. I just can't…"

"Yes, you can."

"How do you know what I was going to say?"

"It doesn't matter. Whatever it is you think you can't do, I know you—we—can. What we have is strong enough to get us past this."

She looked at him, her eyes swelling again with tears. "Why won't you just get on with your life and leave all this—leave me—behind?"

"Because I love you."

She'd wondered what it would feel like to hear those words from him. Now she knew. She thought she might be scared by it and maybe she was, a little. But then she could feel her heart beating faster and a feeling of sheer and utter happiness welling up to catch in her throat. Until 'scared' reared its head again.

"How can you? How can you love someone who would put the person she loves in harm's way?"

His smile was broad and the hopeful look had returned to his face. "The person you love?"

"Nick…"

"Okay, we'll get back to how you feel about me in a minute. Beautiful, sending people to war is putting them in harm's way. Didn't whatever Ken Burns documentary you got the phrase from teach you that? You didn't come close." He put out his hand to her and she sat back down next to him, lacing her fingers through his.

"Why?" she asked.

"Why, what?" He seemed genuinely puzzled at her question.

"Why do you love me?"

His smile was even broader now. "Because I'd never met a woman like you. You don't just accept the surface of anything. You're like Dorothy outing the Wizard, you need to know what's behind the curtain. I love your passion for finding out, your curiosity, your intelligence."

"After what my curiosity did to you?"

"I've apparently failed to say convincingly what I came here to say—what happened to me wasn't your fault. So, I guess I'll call Sam. Maybe he can explain it better."

"Please don't."

"If you won't talk to Sam, at least call my sister. She's been worried sick about you. I thought she was your friend."

"She is. I know I should have called her a long time ago. But I did, today, when I got back from Tacoma. She was in the middle of something and is calling me back."

"Thank God. She's been frantic." He cocked his head and frowned. "Tacoma? You went home to your parents?"

"Yeah. I needed to sort some things out."

"Like?"

"Like returning a robe. And figuring out how to get over being in love with someone I don't deserve."

Nick was quiet for a moment. "Were those two things connected?"

"No. Two different situations. I discovered I didn't really need to hold on to the robe. It was over a long time ago. I've been working on the latter."

"I had a lot of time on the damn cruise ship to think, too. I came back here determined to put the last three weeks behind us." He drew her slowly into his arms. "I want to make this right."

She sighed and rested her head against his chest as he held her. "I feel like I'm in this deep hole. I don't know if it's possible to make it right or get out of it."

"I know we can." He pushed her gently back so he could see her face. "And you had help digging the hole. Sam, me."

"You? What did you do?"

"I should have come here weeks ago. Not coming to your front door is almost worse than failing to rescue you from those thugs."

"Oh, God, Nick. You're so far from being to blame…"

"Neither of us had it right. But we don't have to stay here, stuck in this hole. We can find our way out. Look at me, Fee." He tipped up her chin so she was looking straight into his eyes. He kissed her forehead. "I love you. And you love me. Right now, that's where we start."

Her arms went around his neck almost of their own accord; he lowered his head and their mouths met. It was the sweet, sensuous kiss she'd been able to block out of her waking hours but unable to ban from her dreams. There was tenderness in the kiss and a little regret, passion, and a bit of pain. But most of all there was love.

When it ended he pressed his cheek against her hair, hugged her, then said, "Know what I missed? The smell of your hair. I love the smell of your hair."

"I missed you, too. You're why I rearranged the furniture. I couldn't stand to be here seeing you everywhere. That's part of the reason I stayed in Tacoma so long."

He stroked her face. "I have a slide show on my computer of some of the photos I took of you. Some days I'd look at them over and over. Other days, I couldn't even turn the damn thing on for fear I'd see you."

She touched his face. "I've looked and looked but I can't see a scar anyplace on your face. When you left the mountain, it looked like you were bleeding from everywhere."

"Mostly from a broken nose, apparently, and a couple of cuts. I guess the blood splattered everyplace else. The docs straightened my broken nose so it doesn't show, although I did have an amazing pair of black eyes for a while." He took her hand and ran her forefinger along the bridge of his nose so she could feel the small bump, the only residual of the break.

"No broken ribs? No internal injuries?"

"Fortunately, contrary to my stereotype of skinheads, they didn't wear hobnail boots. Their athletic shoes didn't do more than give me bruises."

"Really?"

"Really. I never got in a schoolyard fight when I was a kid but now, thanks to those guys, I can cross it off my bucket list."

"It's not funny, Nick."

"It wasn't then. It is now."

"I thought Amanda was being kind when she left those messages saying you weren't really hurt. I thought she was just trying to get me to go see you."

"And you didn't because...?"

"I was humiliated by the scene we'd created, angry at Sam yelling at me, angry at myself because I was convinced Sam was right, sure you'd never love me because of it."

"And my multiple phone calls, texts, and emails didn't convince you I did?"

"I told you, I haven't been too happy living with the idea I was getting my story by having the man I loved beat up."

"Would you feel better about it if we rewrote what happened? How about—I was your champion going up against the evil knights?"

She laughed for the first time since she'd found him on her doorstep. "I'd have to send that story back for rewrites. 'Champion?' 'Evil knights?' Pretty cliché, don't you think?"

"Ouch. You're not a kind editor, are you?" He kissed her lightly and she ran her finger over his lips. "Speaking of my mouth..."

"What about it?"

"A while ago, you started to say something about my mouth. What was it?" He was smiling at her, knowing, she was sure, exactly what it was about. So she put her hand on the back of his neck and brought his mouth back to hers in another kiss.

"I'm not sure I get it," he said.

"Then I guess we'll just have to keep doing this," she kissed him lightly, "until you do."

"Have I ever told you what a slow learner I am?"

Afterword

Nick and Fiona's story is the last in the six-book Second Chances series. It's not easy for me to say good-bye to characters—*people*—I've lived with for four years, but they want to get on with their lives now that they found Happily-Ever-After. In case there's some curiosity about what happened to the six couples after I wrote "The End" to each of their love stories, here's what I know about how they made out.

Liz and Collins (*Beginning Again*) haven't gotten around to getting married. There is some doubt they ever will. But they share a home in SW Portland, overlooking the Willamette River where they entertain on a regular basis, throwing dinner parties everyone wants to be invited to. Liz's gallery is one of the top five in the city and Collins has more demand for his sculptures than he has time to create them. He's moving his studio from the Wallowa Mountains to the Willamette Valley so he doesn't have to be away from Liz two weeks out of every month. Liz gave up her motto "I never do anything twice" when she ran out of things to add to Collins's to-do list.

Not much has changed for Sam and Amanda (*Loving Again*) They still live in the house in Alameda. Sam's still a Portland homicide detective. Amanda's still one of the most highly regarded glass artists in the region. Only the kids have changed. Sam's older son is looking forward to college in a couple years, which, Sam was stunned to discover, Amanda's trust will pay for. Even though she's still in grade school, Sam and Amanda's daughter, Kat, is a very fine horsewoman. They're all going to Italy this summer where Amanda will be visiting faculty at a prestigious glass conference. She's nervous. Everyone else is counting the days.

For Tony and Margo (*Together Again*) it's been nothing but change. Tony got his wish—their first-born, who arrived nine months after their much-delayed honeymoon in Hawaii, is named Joseph Salvatore Alessandro. Two years later, baby Grace joined the family. Before either baby arrived, the couple moved off the river to a house in the Hollywood area of Portland with a yard and a good school close by. Tony is now Sam's partner. Margo's being groomed to run for DA when Jeff Wyatt retires, which will be just about the time both kids are in school. She still misses Kiki, who went to California to go to law school and has never come home.

A year after Cynthia and Marius (*Trusting Again*) had their daughter, Rose, they planned one more baby. But they got surprised a second time and had twin boys they named Lucas and Martin. With Marius's beautiful home now overflowing with kids, they went house hunting. The first house they were shown had an existing artist's studio on the property, perfect for Cynthia. They snapped it up. She's represented by a dozen high-end galleries on the West Coast. Thanks to Marius's family in Florida, her work's in resort shops there, too. The coffee business continues to thrive for Marius. He still doesn't buy for Starbucks, but he's the broker for just about everyone else.

Danny and Jake (*Believing Again*) joined the parenthood club with a daughter, Rachel, and a son, Aaron. To her surprise, Danny discovered she wanted to be home with her kids when they were little so she left the Police Bureau. Jake's PTSD is under better control than ever and his thoracic surgery practice is thriving. Both he and Danny volunteer at the Veterans' Medical Services Clinic. Since Danny has been there, the number of women vets coming in for help has tripled. She's taking classes at Portland State so she can be a better counselor and may just end up with her master's in social work.

Nick was partly right about Fiona (*Falling Again*). She was a finalist for a Pulitzer for her White Knight stories, although she didn't win. She took the job in Seattle where she and Nick bought a great condo in Belltown. *Trending Stories*, the website she works for, is one of the top news sources on the web, thanks partly to her reporting. Now the proud owner of a passport, Fiona goes with Nick on some of his assignments, the ones where there's no danger of being shot at. He has a book featuring his work coming out in the next year as well as a second joint exhibit with Amanda. One of these days, they'll get around to having a kid.

More from This Author
(From *Believing Again* by Peggy Bird)

Portland Police Detective Danny Hartmann didn't try to hide her surprise at what she was seeing under the east end of the Hawthorne Bridge, one of the eight that span the Willamette River, linking the two sides of Portland, Oregon. It wasn't the dead body that startled her. If the dead man hadn't been there, she'd still be at home, asleep. What she didn't expect was what else was there — a small, well-hidden city of makeshift shelters and camping tents, inhabited by a population of men sleeping in the cold fall rain that was practically a daily event.

"I thought all the people from these homeless camps had been moved indoors." She looked around and tried to make a quick count. "There must be, maybe, a dozen and half people living here."

"Seventeen, to be precise," Doctor Jake Abrams responded. "And, yes, some people were moved indoors a couple weeks ago when your colleagues came through and shut down the camps after some ass-hat business owner complained. But the number of people who need a place to stay is always bigger than the number of spaces available."

Abrams had made the 911 call that brought the uniformed cops, crime scene techs, and two homicide detectives to the transient camp. "The camps reappear under another bridge as soon as the cops leave," he said. "The current iteration has been in existence for about ten days. I'm surprised you haven't had a complaint about it already."

"Sorry," Danny said. Other than as a reaction to the anger in the doctor's voice, she wasn't sure why she was apologizing. "I wasn't aware the Portland Police Bureau was responsible for creating this." She waved her arms to take in the whole transient city.

"Okay, Doc, let's go take a look." Danny's partner, Detective Sam Richardson, ambled over after talking to the two uniforms who'd responded to the emergency call.

Thank God, Danny thought. Someone to change the subject and shut this jerk up. She hoped her disgust wasn't too evident.

"He's … The body's over there," Abrams said, pointing to a shelter set apart from the rest of the camp. "I found him about six A.M., when I came to make rounds." Leading the two detectives toward what looked like an old plastic drop cloth over some sort of cardboard frame, he continued, "At first, when he didn't respond, I thought he was sleeping off a night of drinking. But then I saw this." They'd reached the structure surrounded by yellow crime scene tape, and he pointed to a series of holes low to the ground on one side that Danny immediately knew were bullet holes. "And when I looked inside, I saw he'd been hit several times in the head and neck and bled out."

"So you knew the man?" Sam asked.

"Yeah, his name is … was … Jim Branson. He's an Army vet. Served almost twelve years. Couple tours in Iraq, one in Afghanistan. Returned stateside about eight or nine months ago after he was wounded and discharged. I met him a couple months after that. Patched him up after a brawl. He had PTSD — post traumatic stress disorder — and … "

"We know that one, Doc. We've seen enough colleagues with it," Sam said.

"Right. Sorry. Too used to having to explain it to civilians, I guess." He ran his fingers through his hair. "He drank too much, got into fights, and didn't take care of himself. I was checking on him because of an infected knife wound in his leg."

"You make rounds on these guys every day?" Danny asked.

"No, I can only get here about once a week." He sounded defensive, as if he knew he should be there more often. Danny felt a flicker of pleasure at making the good doctor uncomfortable.

He continued, "I don't usually treat the guys here, just check up on them if they haven't come back to the clinic for a follow-up. Jim is ... was ... an exception. He asked me to treat him here. So I did."

"And you called as soon as you found him," Sam said.

"Of course I did." Abrams made a face that clearly showed how annoyed he was to be asked the question.

Danny waited, repressing a smirk, anticipating the enjoyment she would get from watching her partner put the pain-in-the-ass doctor in his place. Sam was an expert at managing a witness with a chip on his shoulder.

"Didn't mean anything by it, Doc. Sometimes people try to revive the victim or look around for the perp and don't call right away. Just trying to get a clearer picture of how things happened."

Oh, hell. He's playing mild-mannered Sam. Where's the crusty one I know and love? Danny quickly checked the expressions on the faces of the two men to make sure she hadn't said anything out loud. She was relieved when the conversation went on without interruption.

"Sorry." Jake Abrams actually looked like he meant it. "Shouldn't have snapped at you like that. Guess I'm on edge. This is the third time this has happened."

"Third time what has happened?" Sam asked.

"Third time someone's shot into one of the camps. The other two times, no one reported getting hit."

"I don't remember hearing about drive-bys at a transient camp. Was it reported to us?" Danny asked.

The doctor snorted. "I doubt it. Why would anyone report it? You wouldn't do anything about it."

"Other than try and find out who was doing it, no, I don't imagine we would," she said, glaring at him. "I mean it's not like figuring out shit like this is part of our job or anything. So of course ... "

"Danny," Sam interrupted, "why don't you go talk to the guys who were within hearing range and see what you can find out? I'll stay here with the doc and sort out what he found when he got here."

Danny nodded and walked away, relieved to be out of the orbit of what was, she was sure, the snarkiest doctor — maybe the snarkiest person — in the city of Portland.

Ninety minutes later, she'd talked to most of the residents in the camp, two of whom she was surprised to find were women. No one had seen or heard anything other than a few strange noises that hadn't meant much to anyone.

A few of the inhabitants owned up to sleeping off too much booze. A couple said they'd heard noises that could have been backfires, gunshots, or their memories of combat. Most said there were always strange noises at night around the camp — cars and trucks overhead, people walking nearby, rats running around under the bridge. That made Danny even more grateful than usual that she had a warm, snug apartment to go home to. She hated rats.

She was about to rejoin her partner when Doctor Snark flagged her down.

"We got off on the wrong foot," he said. "I'm sorry. Can we start over?"

She waved off his apology. "Don't worry about it. I'm used to people not being real happy to have the police around. We deal with all sorts in this job."

He grinned and his smile lit up his face. A face that was really quite good-looking, now that she re-considered it. Wide-set blue eyes that looked as deep as the sea, dark hair that fell in waves around his ears and over his forehead, a bit shaggy, like he needed a haircut. Sculpted cheekbones, a strong jaw covered in designer stubble, and a full mouth that looked a hell of a lot better smiling than it had thinned into a line of disapproval. In fact, she couldn't take her eyes off his mouth, now that it was smiling at her. It was full-lipped and luscious looking.

His tall and nicely muscled body wasn't bad either.

"I imagine you do," he said. "I meet some jerks in my work, too. But most of the time I try not to be one. This morning I failed. I apologize." He ran his fingers through his hair. "My only excuse is that I get wrapped around the axle when it comes to these guys … "

"And women."

"You noticed. Yeah, and women. They mean a lot to me. And this has me worried. Like I said, it's not the first time we've had someone shoot into one of the camps. If it's the same person doing the shooting, they're escalating and that raises all sorts of red flags. It concerns me. Big time."

"Mind if I ask why this is so important to you?"

"A lot of the people in these camps are veterans, some from as far back as Vietnam, who've had a hard time coming home. I was in the National Guard. In Iraq." He paused for a moment, his eyes clouded, as if seeing something far away. "I know how it is. I volunteer at a clinic for vets. One of the things we do is try and get them to a place where they can really come home. Every part of them." He stopped again.

"Sounds like a tough job," Danny said to prompt him.

"Someone has to do it. The same government that sends these guys off to fight doesn't always do such a great job of making sure they get back to some sort of normal civilian life afterwards. They do okay for most vets but some guys slip through the cracks. Too many of them, in my opinion."

"You said the camps reappear because people have no place to go. Didn't I read about a VA program that provides rent vouchers for homeless vets?"

He nodded. "There is a program like that. Wouldn't be surprised if some of the guys here have those vouchers. What they don't have is a place to use them. Since the housing bubble burst, rentals are in short supply around Portland. The vouchers don't pay as much as the landlords can get on the open market so they limit the number of units available for the guys to use the vouchers."

"Thanks. That helps me understand what's going on a little better."

He looked down at her. "I guess I owe you one more apology."

Curious, she asked, "And what would this one be for?"

"I apologize for casting aspersions on the organization you work for. Apparently not all cops are disinterested in the problems these folks face."

"No apology needed. I'm sure if you rousted my friends out of their homes I wouldn't be too impressed with you, either."

The grin was back. "I don't think you were too impressed with me even though I wasn't anywhere near your friends' homes."

She shrugged her shoulders and smiled in return. "You could be right, Doctor Abrams."

"As long as we're starting over, it's Jake, Detective Hartmann. And you're ... ?"

"Danny. Happy to re-meet you, Jake." She put out her hand and he shook it, holding on to it longer than necessary.

"Danny? There must be a story behind that." The smile that went with the comment moved from merely attractive to downright sexy.

Dammit, he knew exactly what he was doing by continuing to hold on to her hand. "Not really. I like Danny better than my given name."

"Which is?"

"Danita, if you really have to know." She was not about to confess to trying to be one of the guys when she was a kid by turning the name she didn't much like into a boy's name. Needing to change the subject to something other than her, she grabbed onto the first topic that came to mind. "Speaking of names, I should have thought of this earlier but your last name is familiar. You have relatives who are doctors, too?" She managed to remove her hand from his as she asked her question.

"Generations of them. A tradition on both sides of the family. I followed one grandfather onto the staff at Kaiser. The other grandfather was on the faculty at the medical school. My mother's a pediatrician up at Doernbecher. My brother is a psychiatrist in Vancouver. My father's a surgeon at Emanuel."

"That's it. I think your father was the doc who put Sam back together a few years ago after he got shot up."

"He'll remember if he was. I swear my father can recall the name of everyone he's ever treated. And if Sam was his patient he'll be happy to hear he's doing great. Boosts his ego to hear how well his work turned out."

"Speaking of work, I better get back to mine. We'll be in touch. Promise me that if something, anything, happens that even vaguely seems like it's related to this, you'll call us." Reaching into her pants pocket she pulled out a business card and handed it to him. "My number's on here. If Sam forgets to give you his card, ask for it."

He scrutinized the card. "Hmm. No home address so I can come and roust you out."

"No, Jake. And don't bother with four-one-one. That won't find me either." She smiled before heading to the patrol car where the responding officers were congregated.

167

Damn. Why the hell had he been such an S.O.B. when he first met her? Now she wouldn't give him the time of day — unless it was the time she'd be at her desk, willing to listen to any evidence he might have. That wouldn't be the worst way to get back into her good graces. If only he could find something.

As he watched her walk away, he noticed that the rear view of the very attractive detective was almost as good as the view from the front. She was tall, maybe five-eight, five-nine. And she walked like she owned the place, a long stride with a controlled sway to her hips that wasn't sexual but was surely sensual. And those hips and fine ass were covered by chocolate brown pants that fit like a glove. The cream-colored shirt she wore looked good with her honey blonde hair and bourbon-colored eyes.

Where the hell were all the food images coming from? He wasn't hungry; he'd eaten breakfast that morning. Maybe not enough. Or maybe it was that he thought the lady looked good enough to eat. Although, she had a mouth on her that made him certain she'd be no lady when she was in charge of who was eating what.

He shook his head to stop this disastrous train of thought. The image of Danny Hartmann, on her knees in front of him, deciding who was eating whom, had to go before it took up residence in his head and distracted him for the rest of the day. He had surgeries waiting for him. Even food metaphors describing her hair and eyes were better than the very pleasurable image of her naked that was filling his thoughts and making his mouth dry.

"You okay, Doc?" Sam Richardson interrupted his fantasizing, looking concerned.

If Sam only knew how not okay Jake's thoughts about his partner were, he'd be more than concerned. "Yeah, I'm fine." Jake shook his head again, trying to clear it. "You finished talking to people?"

"Mostly. For now anyway. The patrol officers are about to leave. Danny and I will be around for another half hour or so. If you need to get to the clinic … "

"Nope, on my way to the hospital. I'm in surgery for most of the day but if you need me, here's my number." He pulled out his own card, tucking Danny's into his wallet as he did so. "Leave a message and I'll get back to you between cases."

"Sounds good. Is that Danny's card? I'll give you mine, too." Sam handed him a business card and looked as if he was about to walk away.

"Ah, Detective Richardson? One more thing, not related to what happened here. It's personal and I'll understand if you don't want to answer."

"Okay, what is it?" Richardson sounded very curious and a bit wary.

"It's about Detective Hartmann … Danny. Is she attached?"

"Attached? If you mean professionally, yeah, she is. To me. She's my partner. But if you mean personally, the only attachment I know of is to the classic VW convertible she restored and rebuilt from the engine out."

"Wow."

"Yup. That about covers it. She's a 'wow' kind of woman."

Sam had a look on his face that said he wanted to say — or ask — more, but he didn't, much to Jake's relief. Jake wasn't even really sure why he'd asked about her. It wasn't like there was a chance she'd be interested. Not after the way he'd behaved when they first met.

Fortunately, Sam merely shook his hand and walked away. Jake got out of there as fast as he could, kicking himself for behaving like an idiot, first with Danny, now with her partner. He needed to lose himself in his work.

Also from this author, check out:

Beginning Again

Loving Again

Together Again

Trusting Again

In the mood for more Crimson Romance?
Check out *Hiding From Hollywood* by Ellie Darkins at
CrimsonRomance.com.